FATAL FESTIVITIES: A CHRISTMAS MYSTERY NOVELLA

PARTNERS IN SPYING MYSTERIES

ROSE DONOVAN

Moon Snail Press

Fatal Festivities

Copyright © 2021 by Rose Donovan

www.rosedonovan.com

Published by Moon Snail Press

Editing: The Hackney Fiction Doctor & Heddon Publishing

All rights reserved. No part of this book may be reproduced or transmitted in any form or by any means, electronic or mechanical, including photocopying, recording, or by any information storage and retrieval system without the written permission of the author and publisher.

All the characters in this book are fictitious, and any resemblance to actual persons living or dead is purely coincidental.

Cast of Characters at Cavendish Mansions

Ruby Dove – Student of chemistry at Oxford, fashion designer, and amateur spy-sleuth. On a mission to right injustices.

Fina Aubrey-Havelock – Student of history at Oxford, assistant seamstress to Ruby, and her best friend. Ready to defend Ruby, at any cost.

Pixley Hayford – A shameless journalist on the hunt for a scoop. Always game for a Ruby and Fina adventure, especially if it involves a possible story.

Lady Lavinia Charlesworth – Patron of the arts and host of the soirée. Giles Lechmere-Slade is her current lover.

Giles Lechmere-Slade – Gentleman friend of Lady Charlesworth. Fancies himself a suave man-of-the-world and an excellent dancer.

Ruth Croscombe – A born organiser and long-time friend of Lady Charlesworth and Nigel Shrimpton. A dangerously efficient soul.

Professor Eldred Wharton – Stepfather to Vincent Avery. Rex Camden is his research assistant. A great scholar and humanitarian.

Beale – Devilishly handsome butler to Lady Charlesworth. A most peculiar chap.

Rex Camden – Saxophone player in the Dizzy Blighty jazz trio. Ambitious and fastidious.

Hattie El Nadi – Elfin girl about town with an eye toward romance in every direction. Best friend of Edith Lin's. Or is she?

Edith Lin – Niece of Lady Charlesworth and cousin to Nigel Shrimpton. Engaged to Vincent Avery and best friend of Hattie El Nadi's. Quiet and very clearly determined.

Silas Marsh – Drummer in Dizzy Blighty, with a rather drippy personality.

Vincent Avery – Piano player in Dizzy Blighty and Professor Wharton's stepson. An amiable fiancé to Edith Lin, but does he have a wandering eye?

Nigel Shrimpton – Shrimpy by name, but not by nature. Nephew of Lady Charlesworth and cousin to Edith Lin. A crashing bore of a rugger player.

Chief Inspector Radford – An owlish detective without imagination, but not without certain flexibility.

George & Millie Taney – Landlords of the Toddling Otter inn in Surrey.

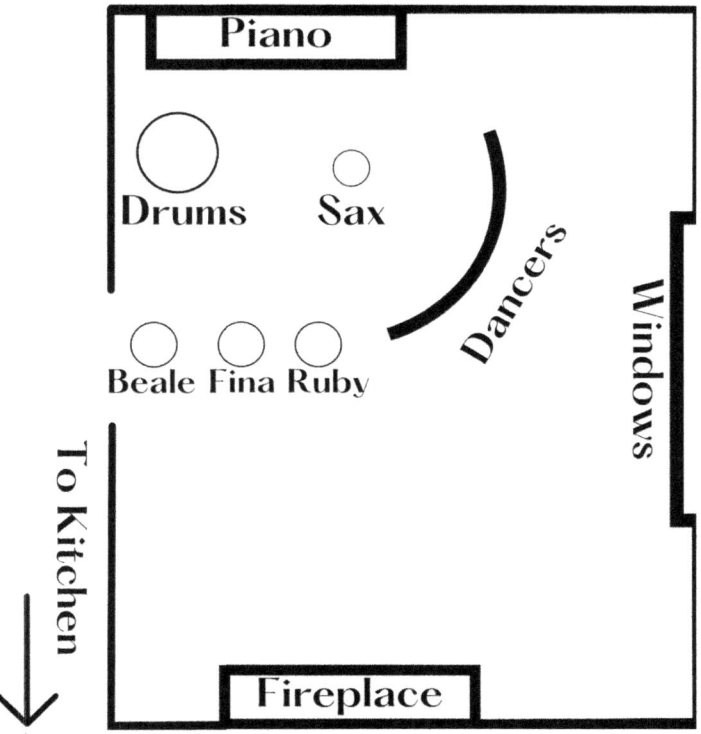

The Collision at Lady Charlesworth's

1

I shall always look upon our fatal festivities case with fondness. Calling it a 'case' may be a bit far-fetched, but I hope the dear reader agrees it has the necessary elements of a mystery – intrigue, a puzzle, and, naturally, a murder. Whilst that might be sufficient for an average reader, it's not for me. I need a detective. A detective I can believe in. Miss Ruby Betto Dove.

A LOUD SNAP echoed from the corridor. I glanced at my watch. Ten o'clock was a bit early for the post, but perhaps one of Ruby's bohemian friends had dispatched sketch ideas for her new line of gowns.

I rose from the overstuffed chair, wiggling my toes near the crackling fire and mantel I'd adorned with holly and ivy for Christmas. Reluctant to leave the fireside on this cold, grey London morning, I nevertheless padded past the wooden chairs of varied heights, past the blue and black painting of a fisherwoman in St Kitts, and finally past the dress form, a necessary presence in Ruby Dove's flat. Earlier in the week, I'd draped a wool jumper over the naked form, and was pleased that it, too, looked as snug as my covered toes.

An ordinary envelope lay folded on the bristle mat near the front door. I inspected the sealed flap and turned it over, but the missive was curiously devoid of address or name.

The cold draught from the door prickled the hairs on my arms, so I hurried back to the sitting room and threw a fluffy wool shawl around my shoulders. I flipped the letter over and over again, considering my dilemma. Before she'd left for a student conference last week, Ruby had instructed me to read all important post.

Nothing thus far had risen to the level of 'importance', but this looked different. Dash it. Time to take action. I tore open the envelope and slid the single sheet of cheap paper from inside. It read: "Lady Charlesworth's soirée, December 18th, at 9 o'clock."

The downstairs bell buzzed in three short bursts, and for the second time that morning, I jumped. Slipping and then regaining my balance on the wooden floor, I ran to the window. I rubbed the foggy pane and peered at the streetlamp's anaemic light struggling to banish the grey day. A shiny red sports car burst through the sepia background of the street. The motorcar must have cost the owner a pretty penny.

Pressing my nose against the pane, I strained my eyes towards the entrance to Ruby's building. Not a soul stirred, not even a – well, perhaps a flapping pigeon.

"Fina! I'm home!"

Ruby Dove leaned against the doorframe, resplendent in her grey travelling suit and upswept raven hair. Her favourite opal pinprick earrings peeked out from her navy beret, and her eyebrows, though not over-plucked as was the fashion, framed her broad doe eyes with a hint of the sardonic.

"I rang the bell to avoid surprising you. Though it seems I've failed in that task."

"Not at all. I had a late night, so I woke only an hour ago." I adjusted my shawl, grimacing at my own slovenly appearance. A glance in the looking glass confirmed that my fringe stood on end, as if it were an auburn tidal wave ready to crash onto my forehead.

Ruby pulled off her gloves, finger by finger. "A late night? Involving delicious debauchery, I hope?"

"Sadly, it involved nothing more debaucherous than a box of chocolates and a gripping detective novel – *The Clue of the Fourth Hedgehog*."

Ruby shivered and slid her folded gloves into her pocket. "Not my cup of tea, I'm afraid."

"Ah, I had forgotten. Your fear of hedgehogs, I mean." Seizing the opportunity to wipe the distress from Ruby's face, I pointed at the missive lying on the chair. "Talking of which, this mysterious note just arrived in the post. Or, rather, someone pretended it was the post. I wish I could say it was a jolly Christmas card, but it's nothing of the sort."

Ruby laid her beret lovingly on the dress form's neck – fashionably askew – and settled into a wooden chair with tall legs. I had attempted the same earlier and found I was swinging my legs like a child. The seventeenth-century chair was better suited to my frame. I would have been a positive giant if I had been born a few hundred years ago.

She looked up from the letter, her perfectly framed eyebrows clearing from a V-like position of exaggerated vexation. "I've received several of these notes instructing me to be at a certain place at a certain time. Frankly, I've ignored them as childish pranks."

A lorry rumbled past the window, reminding me of what I'd seen on the street. "Before I forget, do you know anything about the red motorcar outside? You haven't had a sudden fancy to take up driving, have you?"

"Ha!" She thumped her hand on the chair. "That'd be a laugh. Can you imagine it? I'd be so concerned about scratches and dints that I'd be unable to drive around the block. No, it's Pixley's new motorcar – his pride and joy."

"Where is he, then?"

"He popped round to the shop for fresh buns. He loves the ones near the park." She paused. "And I can see you love them, too, if that noise from your stomach is any indication."

"Sadly, my stomach is distracted, but my brain is determined to focus on your secret messages. Why have you ignored them? Who's writing them?"

Ruby tapped her teeth. "At first, I thought someone in the African Student Union sent them – as a way of asking me to undertake a mission relating to their, ah, activities."

I nodded, recalling our many adventures in pursuit of justice. Although Ruby's sense of injustice was much keener than mine, allowing her to understand people's often bizarre motivations.

"But then?" I asked.

"But then I inquired with the ASU chair, and he hadn't a clue about their origin. I even gave him a wink and a nudge, but he continued to deny any knowledge about them."

"Perhaps it's an ASU member acting on their own?"

She shook her head. "I asked around, and Pixley even queried his journalist chums at the *Daily Correspondent*."

I heard the front door open and shut. A delectable, doughy smell of hot buns soon filled the flat. "Well, there's only one thing to do, dear Ruby." I rose and shuffled towards the door. "As the arrival of these lovely buns requires all my attention, we must come to a decision."

Ruby grimaced. "You mustn't say it."

"But I must," I said, twirling around in my slippers. "We shall go to the ball!"

2

The following Friday, we shambled up the wide steps to Cavendish Mansions; a large, modern block of flats. I say 'shambled' because we struggled up the stairs, weighed down by our load and a stiff wind. My hair flitted across my face.

"Pix, could you ring the bell? My hands are full. I wonder why the commissionaire hasn't already opened the door." As I lifted my head, trying to dislodge the strands of hair, my lovely new blue Florentine hat slid onto the damp stones. I twisted and turned, still grasping two cold bottles of bubbly.

"I cannot ring the blasted bell, either." Pixley lifted one knee and steadied the wooden box on it. "Jupiter's teeth. Why the devil do we need all these champagne bottles, Ruby?"

"Lady Charlesworth requested them when I rang her. Remember, silly goose?" Ruby pushed my hat back onto my head and pressed the button.

Pixley adjusted his round, black-framed spectacles. "Maybe she's playing at being a bohemian of sorts. Because if she's *a lady* and lives in such swanky quarters, surely she can afford her own alcohol."

"Not at the rate some of us drink it," I laughed, smiling at

Pixley. Though Pixley Hayford could certainly imbibe more than was good for him, he still maintained a steady hand. Perhaps it was his stocky figure and muscles straining through the sleeves of his well-cut suit. Or perhaps it was his profession, as journalists were a hard-drinking lot. Merely a quarter of what he could drink made me squiffy. In fact, I was looking forward to becoming perfectly squiffy after another gruelling term at Oxford and my week of solitude at Ruby's flat. It was Christmastime, after all.

Ruby adjusted her own slanting-brim hat and pressed the bell again. "I see you're wearing your favourite red jumper, Pix. The one Madame Zora gave you when we were in Italy. Very festive."

Pixley caressed the delicate red wool. "It's positively magnetic – for certain kinds of people, that is." He winked at us. "You two look spiffing yourselves. That vivid green suits your auburn hair, Feens. And Ruby's wine frock is mellow and wise, just like the wearer."

"Go on with you, Mr Hayford," chirped Ruby.

The door swung open. A pink-faced man with a cap and a white, mushrooming goatee scowled at us. I half expected a parrot on his shoulder and a pipe in his mouth. He was hardly the grand commissionaire you'd expect in this mansion block for London society types.

I followed Ruby's lead, stepping forwards over the threshold. Close up, the man had a map of broken red capillaries spread across his nose, scrunched in disapproval as his eyes bored into Ruby and Pixley.

My fingers tingled and my nose twitched.

As if sensing my rising anger, Ruby waved our missive at the commissionaire. "We have an invitation to Lady Charlesworth's event. I'm Miss Ruby Dove, and this is Fina Aubrey-Havelock and Pixley Hayford. Would you notify her of our arrival?"

The man pursed his fleshy lips and held out a hand for the note. But he jerked backwards quickly at a low warning growl, coming from somewhere deep in my belly. Much like the warm red flush in my face that was a constant companion, it was a bodily reaction I had little control over.

He wagged a finger sprouting with tufts of hair in Ruby's face. "We do not allow pets in this building, miss."

Pixley placed a hand on Ruby's shoulder and hoisted himself up, even though he could barely peek over her. "That growl is not a dog, sir. It's my dear friend, Miss Aubrey-Havelock."

I could see little point in denying it and was so incensed by our treatment that I pushed past the commissionaire into the foyer. The plush surroundings were lined with an assortment of insipid paintings of wealthy women with their tiny dogs. I jabbed the lift button, and waved to Ruby and Pixley.

They hurried past the spluttering commissionaire and leapt into the lift. He grabbed the telephone receiver on his desk – undoubtedly to call some other officious oaf – just as the door closed.

The whir of the elevator faded as Pixley doubled over in a fit of giggles. "Dear Feens, you must become a journalist if this clothing business or academic career fails to bear fruit. You're as bold as the devil. The look on that blighter's face!"

Ruby's eyes crinkled. "It was marvellous. And come Christmas morning I'm certain he'll find a lump of coal in his stocking."

With a jolt, we landed on the fifth floor. Shrieks and screams met our ears as we opened the lift door.

"What on earth is that din?" I asked, my feet sinking into the thick green mat welcoming us to number 51. "Is someone being murdered?"

"Just good clean fun," said Pixley. He handed Ruby a bottle

of bubbly and pressed yet another bell. "Well, perhaps not strictly clean, but that's neither here nor there."

Heavy footsteps approached, clear even amidst the terrific noise coming from within. Ruby whispered, "Remember, we're here for a jolly time, but also to discover who invited us, and why."

I didn't need a reminder, though perhaps I would after my first cocktail.

The door was flung open with such force that it blew back the long, looping pearl necklace of our greeter. A solidly built, matronly figure grinned from ear to ear as if the good God had cut the corners of her mouth further than most. Her imposing bulk, looming like a snorting bull, suggested one of Bertie Wooster's alarming aunts, but her delightful clothing and warm voice gave the opposite impression. Her shimmering silver skirt and black top set off her pearls and décolletage. The dated feathered contraption on her head, circa 1918, only added to her charm.

"Darlings, do come in!" She held her arms wide. "And I must apologise for our frightful commissionaire, as I'm sure he was quite rude to you. Rather stuck in his ways, I'm afraid. But you'll feel at home here, I assure you."

Ruby held up a bottle of champagne. "We're ever so grateful for your invitation, Lady Charlesworth. Shall we place these bottles in your kitchen?"

Lady Charlesworth held up her hands to her face in horror, as if she had committed the faux pas of the century. "But of course, of course!" She snapped her fingers and a man who could only be described as tall, dark, and handsome materialised beside her. Winking at us, he ran a hand over his slicked-back hair and snapped up our bottles. He turned on his heel and was swallowed up in the crowd.

I glanced at Pixley, already anticipating his reaction. He

stammered, mouth agape, "Who is your butler – or is he a manservant?"

Lady Charlesworth leaned in and intoned in a deep, almost raspy voice, "He is rather delicious, isn't he? His name is Beale. 'Bewitching' is what I call him privately. Came to me a few months ago on a recommendation from a dear friend."

Then she grabbed Ruby's hand and pulled her across the hall into the drawing room, zigzagging through the tightly packed crowd of people of all ages, sizes, and styles of dress. I found it enchanting, if not bewildering. In my admittedly short-lived experience with such gatherings, these parties invariably featured the same type – mostly young, attractive, and if not wealthy in their bank account, surely possessing relatives with ample allowances for their Bright-Young-Thing existence.

Pixley dashed headlong into the crowd, crying, "Follow the feather!" as I struggled through the sardine tin much less gracefully than my two friends.

"Sorry, pardon, excuse me," I parroted many times after treading on several toes and elbowing at least three unfortunate guests. Then, as I approached the fireplace near a large Christmas tree in the corner, a terrific pain shot up my leg.

3

I gazed at a large black brogue covering my darling white evening shoe.

Bother. My new heels were ruined.

"I'm frightfully sorry. I'm such an oaf," said a florid young man with a broad nose and an even broader smile. His muscles strained against his ill-fitting jacket, recalling Pixley's physique. Though I guessed that was about all they had in common.

"At least that's what my mother says," he continued, transferring a piece of chocolate cake to his left hand. He wiped his fingers on his tailored sleeve and stuck it out towards me, hitting me in the ribs. "I must apologise. Have I ruined your shoes? I can be such a perfect ass."

Whilst my shoe's angry streak-marks inclined me to agree with his assessment, I took his hand and winced as he crushed mine in a powerful grip.

"Good Lord, I've done it again." He pulled back his hand and shook it, scolding his own appendage. "Forgive me. The name's Nigel. Nigel Shrimpton. Though my chums call me Shrimpy."

"Well, Nigel Shrimpton," I said, forgoing any name jokes, "you are almost as clumsy as I am – Fina Aubrey-Havelock, by the way – so I can scarcely be upset given how many trodden-on toes I've left in my wake."

Nigel's grin revealed a set of large, neat, round teeth. Rather unusually well kept, even if they indicated a continuous desire to eat – something else we had in common.

"I say, you're awfully sporting and all that. It's jolly kind to make me feel better about myself. My rugger mates can be, well, rather harsh on a chap – even though I scored two tries yesterday."

I sighed, glancing around to see if anyone could rescue me from this scintillating conversation. Lady Charleston's taste was eclectic without being overstuffed. Colourful oil paintings dotted the walls, but the furniture and upholstery were simple and streamlined, creating a warm yet calming effect. And though the Christmas tree's appearance was a little early in the season, its shining glass baubles managed to be festive yet tasteful. After all, I had already decorated Ruby's flat with holly and ivy.

"Just the other day, Digby Richards said, 'Shrimpy, you're the stupidest player I've ever seen'..."

Shrimpy droned on about his horrid mates and I continued to scan the room, seeking a rescuer, or at least a drink. Even the Shrimpies of this world could be endured if one had a proper cocktail.

Everyone had their backs to me, so I fixed my eyes on the large gilt looking glass to my right, squinting from the occasional flash of a light turned off or on. Guests waged a battle over mood lighting, but the forces of blessed darkness won, and the lights lowered. Now candlelight illuminated the beads of rain dripping on the panes outside.

"Then, the next day, wouldn't you know..." Nigel interrupted himself and inhaled a stack of finger sandwiches from his pyramid of stockpiled food. My ever-active stomach growled, so

I distracted myself by staring into the looking glass once more. An older gentleman with a King Charles-style handlebar moustache winked back at me.

Really. I was a hopeless case if the only attention I could garner in a dimly lit room full of tipsy revellers was a sweet but dull rugby player and a man as old as my grandfather. Sighing, I turned back to Nigel, now leaning against a bookshelf and staring at the ceiling as he rambled about his various nicknames. His cocktail glass perched near his elbow, which was inching closer and closer. I opened my mouth, but it was too late. Red liquid sprayed across Nigel's jacket, followed by the inevitable tinkle on the floor.

My face flamed, as if I had been responsible for the mishap. Even amidst the din, all heads turned and stared at us, but the laughter and hum of the crowd soon returned, thankfully.

A woman buzzed towards us with a brush and dustpan, like a bumblebee who'd spotted her favourite flower. "Nigel, dear, you really can be a perfect oaf."

Nigel sighed. "It's true, Ruth... it's just what..."

"I know, it's just what your mother says." Ruth bent over the shards of glass and swept them into the dustpan. "I ought to know – she is my best friend."

An image of a Women's Institute army loomed before me. Ruth's motherly, fussy style was even more out of place at this swanky London bash than Nigel. Her attempt at a shingle hairstyle had gone awry, though the result was a pleasant golden halo that quivered when she spoke.

"I'm so pleased to meet you, I'm sure," she said once Nigel had introduced us. "I'm Ruth Croscombe, mother of two little darling boys, Tommy and Timmy. Tommy is six and Timmy is eight. I'm not normally in London, but we did take the train especially from Woking. Lavinia – Lady Charlesworth – is a dear old family friend, and when I heard Nigel would be here too, I simply had to make arrangements. Must keep busy!" Her words tumbled out so quickly I was certain she'd also need to sweep them up from the floor.

When she paused to inhale, I blurted, "A pleasure to meet you as well. Do you always travel with a dustpan?"

Ruth looked down at the brush. "This old thing?" she said as if she were talking about last season's Chanel. "Always pays to be prepared. That's what I say. Just the other day, I was telling my Aunt Beatrice, I said, 'Aunt Beatrice...'"

This was proving more insipid than Nigel's ramblings, so I nearly shrieked when I heard the beloved word: "Feens?"

Ruby's eyes twinkled with just a touch of mischief. She clearly enjoyed rescuing me from the jaws of motherly proverbs.

"I'm absolutely gasping for a drink, Ruby. Do you think you could—?"

On cue, Pixley pressed a blessed pink cocktail into my hand. I threw my head back and downed it in one gulp.

"Well, I..." trailed off Ruth in a half-admiring, half-censorious tone.

Ruby took firm hold of my arm. "Please do forgive us, Mrs, ah, but I must introduce my friend to some special guests." Grasping my arm, she piloted me through the maze of writhing bodies into a relatively quiet corridor. A couple cuddling in the doorway ignored us as we trotted past.

"That could be you, Red," Pixley whispered behind me. He was the only person who called me 'Red' after my hair – and possibly my cheeks' tendency to flame at a moment's notice. He was also the only one allowed to call me by such a name.

I turned and gave Pixley a playful punch in the arm.

Except it wasn't Pixley. Beale's grey eyes stared back at me in amusement, though his mouth was set in a grim line. He held a gleaming silver candlestick in his hand.

"Oh, I am frightfully sorry... you see, I thought you were my friend," I said, pointing to Pixley, who shook his head sadly, as if I were a predictably pathetic creature.

Beale lifted the candlestick over my head, and for a moment I quailed – but with a quick motion, he held it up to the light. "I was just polishing the silver, miss." He wiped its base with a handkerchief, removing an imaginary mark.

Behind Beale, Pixley shrugged and held up his hands, continuing his mime act. I had to agree with him – this Beale was an odd character. Perhaps he had been hit with a candlestick as a child. Or perhaps he had been in the war? No, he was much too young for that.

"Ah, yes, well, carry on, Beale," I said, slinking away in a backward, crab-like motion. "We must be on our way." I gestured behind me and dashed into the next room.

Ruby sat near a table piled high with dishes and half-full drinks glasses. A tower of dishes leaned at a perilous angle in the kitchen sink, giving the room a slightly sour odour.

"Beale is peculiar, isn't he?" she said. "Though dishy."

"I'll say," I said. "Looked like he was about to cosh me with that candlestick."

She waved away a fly determined to attack a half-empty glass of egg-nog. "No, I meant why is he polishing the silver when he obviously hasn't set foot in the kitchen to clean up this horror?"

Clapping her hands together, she continued. "But that's not what I'm keen to discuss. Pixley and I had a rather engaging conversation with Lady Charlesworth whilst you were plying your charms against that florid young man. He is Lady Charlesworth's nephew, by the way."

Pixley ambled in, munching on a cheese straw. "Dear Ruby pumped the old bird for all she was worth."

"You've been watching too many films again, Pix," I said, liberating a chair of three teacups. "And I'll have you know I was desperate to escape that dreadful Shrimpy."

Pixley's eyebrows rose. "Who? Lady C's nephew? He's called Shrimpy?"

"His name is Nigel Shrimpton."

"Say no more. I am well acquainted with the curious nicknaming practices of young men. An acquaintance of mine once tried to call me Harry Pate, as in H-a-i-r-y."

"I'm sure you put a stop to that at once," said Ruby.

"He leapt from the category of acquaintance into that of stranger."

The fly zipped along the edge of the egg-nog glass, still holding Ruby's attention.

"Ruby?" I said. "Has our mysterious invitation-writer been revealed?"

She looked at me, and then at Pixley. "Sorry, it was just something you said about a stranger, Pix. It jogged my memory."

I tapped my foot. "Spill the beans. What did Lady Charlesworth say?"

Seeing that Ruby was still distracted, Pixley said, "She expected Professor Eldred Wharton tonight, but she just received a wire that customs had detained him at the airport."

"Who's he when he's at home?" I asked.

Pixley sighed. "Ruby must have mentioned him – he's a visiting scholar from Trinidad. More of a roving scholar, really. He actually trained as a chemist, like Ruby, but dabbles in literature and history. Right up your alley with the history, Red."

I blinked. "Never heard of him, and though I have a strong memory for faces, names are not included." I moved closer to Ruby, almost afraid to break her trance. "Do you think he invited you?"

"No, though he might be the reason we're supposed to be here," she said.

"You mean he's supposed to supply you with vital information?"

"Perhaps. His stepson, Vincent Avery, has already arrived with two women-friends in tow. He might be the letter-writer, especially since he lives in London, unlike his stepfather."

Pixley looked at his watch. "It's 10 o'clock. Lady C also said that Professor Wharton's student, Rex Camden, ought to have arrived by now to 'liven up the party', as she said."

I snorted. "And how's this young man supposed to liven up the party?"

"He's a saxophone player with the Dizzy Blighty jazz trio. Hot stuff, according to the old Charlesworth. And this Vincent cove is the piano player." Pixley banged on the back of his chair. "Time to stir your stumps. In fact, since you two prefer talk over action, I appoint myself Lord of Misrule."

"Pardon?" Ruby and I said in unison.

Pixley threw his shoulders back. "You know, that Christmas tradition where you appoint someone to be the Lord of Misrule – the person who gets to decide what the group will do next."

Ruby giggled. "You certainly are our Lord of Misrule, Pix."

"Thank you, Peasant Dove." He held his nose high in the air. "Now, the jazz trio is bound to start any minute in the other room and our cosy banter won't help us find the author of those letters. Time for action, my fearless friends."

As if on cue, the lights flickered and plunged the room into complete darkness.

4

A grinding thump broke the silence.

Rising murmurs gained speed, as if a lowered curtain had signaled the beginning of an intermission. Shuffling and scraping noises came from my left, though I was uncertain if they were from inside the kitchen or the corridor.

"Feens – do you have a light?" hissed Ruby.

"You know I don't smoke, but Pixley does." I paused, waiting for Pixley's response. "Pix? Are you there?"

"Pix?" I said again.

Ruby whispered, "Here, take my hand." With her on one side, I traced the wall with my fingertips. "I can see a candle glowing from the next room."

As the lights flashed on, I blinked in the harsh light. Ruby poked her head into the corridor. "Pixley? What happened to you? Why'd you leave us?"

Pixley padded around the corner. "I remembered Beale had placed a torch on a table in the corridor, just after we arrived – but it disappeared."

"That Beale is terribly busy with maintenance projects," said Ruby, "but not when it comes to electrical wiring."

A booming voice echoed from the drawing room, followed by two rapid claps, so we hastened back to where Lady Charlesworth was holding court.

"Darlings. Please forgive our brief interruption – we've been having difficulties with the electricity all week, as my long-suffering friends know." She gestured to Beale. "But the party must continue. Beale will roll back the rugs, and we'll dance the night away!"

Claps and whistles ensued as Beale dutifully rolled back the large, soft rugs into a corner. Next to me, an elfin creature with a short dark bob bounced up. Her flame-red chiffon frock swished as she began flipping through the record collection. Another girl in white silk took tentative steps towards the gramophone, as if it might bite.

The elf held up a record to my nose. Her flat, down-tilted eyebrows belied her obvious delight with her find. "Shall we try *Rug Cutter's Swing*?"

"Oh, yes, I'm sure that will be wonderful." Inane replies were apparently my speciality tonight.

She frowned and put down the record, as if my affirmative reply meant the opposite. I tried not to feel offended, but I had the sensation of being in school again under the critical gaze of the popular girls.

Her friend in white silk peered down her long nose and sorted through the records one by one, as if ready to catalogue them in the library should the need arise.

The elf sniffed. "Edith, embrace the spirit of the thing! Try selecting one at random. Even if it's slow, we'll have an excuse to dance rather cosily with someone."

"Right, Hattie. I'll do my best," replied Edith in a flat tone. She continued her systematic progress, ignoring her friend's instructions.

"Hattie, can't you see the crowd's itching to dance?" said a young man. He drummed his fingers on her hand. "The trio will start in a moment – we're just waiting on Rex to warm up."

He turned to Edith. "Find anything with fizz, darling?"

Edith flinched and brushed her hand against her black chignon. "Still searching, Vince." This must be Vincent, stepson of Professor Wharton. He had the long fingers of a piano player, and the loose limbs of a dancer. The few freckles dotting his long nose were the only distinctive feature of an otherwise conventionally handsome face.

Edith glanced at Vincent and then glared at Hattie, though I couldn't tell if it was from hatred, jealousy, or perhaps simple irritability. I sensed a developing triangle of sorts.

Hattie threw her arms around Vincent and stared into his cool green eyes, apparently in response to this dare. Just as I thought she'd plant a kiss on Vincent's squashable lips, she released him and skipped across the dance floor. The crowd parted, and I saw several heads turn in her direction.

"She's a lively one, isn't she?" whispered Pixley in my ear. "Shouldn't wonder if she stirs up trouble wherever she goes."

"I disapprove of such women," I sniffed, sounding like my great aunt Cicely, who had a fine line in disapproval. Aunt Cicely even disapproved of my auburn hair, which she had once dubbed 'rather vulgar'.

"Oh, go on." Pixley gave me a nudge in the ribs. "You must admit you're a teensy bit jealous of how she moves with total abandon."

"When I move with total abandon, everything around me abandons me – including overturned chairs and spilled drinks."

After *Rug Cutter's Swing* came to a close, I spotted Ruby and Lady Charlesworth slinking behind a large wooden screen in the corner of the room. Beale followed, disappearing and then reappearing with a grin.

The sultry notes of a saxophone and a brush against a drum

filled the room whilst Beale folded back the large wooden screen hiding the musicians. A tinkling piano jumped in, creating a full-bodied sound so different from the tinny gramophone. Though the pianist and drummer grinned at the crowd as the song crescendoed, the saxophone player's puckered eyes and the taut corners of his mouth sent a little shiver down my neck. This must be Professor Wharton's student.

A hand on my shoulder interrupted my study of the handsome saxophonist. Perhaps it would be Beale? He would be rather a dreamy dance partner. Not quite like the saxophonist, but certainly better than Shrimpy.

But it was not meant to be. Instinctively, I knew the booming voice must be the man with the ridiculous moustache who'd winked at me earlier. He bowed and held out his hand, as if he were about to propose marriage. "I'm Giles Lechmere-Slade, a good friend of Lady Charlesworth's. Would you care to dance?"

Mr Lechmere-Slade's moustache drooped at my rather obvious glances around the room, seeking yet another rescue party. But Pixley's head happily bobbed next to Ruth Croscombe's, whose blonde hair quivered in response. Bless Pixley for dancing with her. On second look, I saw they made quite the pair; Ruth had obviously enjoyed dancing in her younger days. The two had slipped effortlessly into lockstep and their loose limbs flew about without a care.

Ruby was another matter, however. She was dancing two feet away from Nigel Shrimpton and his two left feet.

I shook myself, wiggled my face, and put on my best little-girl smile. "Delighted, Mr Lechmere-Slade." My hooked arm sat at an angle more appropriate to a stroll in the park.

"Giles, please, Miss, ah—" He grabbed my waist and pushed me onto the dance floor.

I gasped for air. "I'm Fina. Where on earth—"

He pulled me tight against his barrel chest. "A pleasure to meet you, Fina. You were about to ask where I learned to dance."

"Well, I—" He pressed his cheek against mine and thrust out our arms, straight ahead and locked together. A familiar warm feeling flushed my cheeks. Without a glance around the room, I could tell all eyes were on us. Of course, choosing the tango amidst a crowd dancing the Charleston and foxtrot was certain to draw attention. The crowd had parted and quieted, though thank goodness Dizzy Blighty played on, oblivious to my plight.

"I lived in Argentina for a spell. Investor in oil and all that nonsense. Loved the place and would have stayed if..." As we reached the doorway, he whipped around to face the other way and pressed against me again, beginning our march back towards a soppily grinning Ruby and Pixley. Even the vivacious Hattie had stopped to watch, though Edith kept an envious eye on her from across the room.

Giles and I came to a halt in the middle of the dancefloor, where he bent me back from the waist with a flourish. I found myself staring upside down at Nigel Shrimpton's brogues, as blood rushed to my ears.

The shouts and applause were deafening as I came back upright. Giles bowed and I followed suit, smiling and edging my way towards the archway, where I ran headlong into Beale. The orange juice he carried on a tray wobbled and sprayed droplets onto my gown and the floor.

"Pardon me, miss," he said, his gloved hands steadying the glass. "Let me fetch a tea towel for you."

"I'm frightfully sorry – I wasn't looking ahead of me. Could I take the glass for you whilst you find a tea towel for the floor?"

"I'll take it, Feens," said Ruby behind me. "You can freshen up your gown."

Beale nodded and pointed at the trio. "Thank you, Miss Dove. The gentleman playing the piano requested the orange juice. He said to set it atop the piano, with proper protection underneath, of course."

Leaving Ruby behind, I arrived at the queue for the smallest room. Edith stood with her arms crossed at the front of the queue. Damn and blast it. I looked back towards the drawing room, wondering if I ought to ask Lady Charlesworth if I could repair my gown elsewhere. Lo and behold, Lady Charlesworth glided down the corridor like the Queen Mary.

"Dear Miss Aubrey-Havelock, but where did you learn to dance like that? It was marvellous! Now everyone is trying to mimic you." She lowered her voice. "And all rather miserable failures, I'm afraid. Though dear Giles is gamely giving a few chaps lessons. My nephew, Nigel, was his first student."

"I wish I could claim credit, but I'm quite clumsy. Mr Lechmere-Slade is so powerful he could probably dance with a trained bear just as well."

"You're too modest, young lady. I know modesty is an English habit, but it won't do for young girls to indulge in it. Take it from me – that's how I found Giles." Lady Charlesworth twinkled.

"I'm sorry. He said you were friends. Are you, well..." I trailed off, disconcerted by someone so old having a lover. She must have been at least fifty.

"I know dear, you were about to say, 'How can someone so old have a gentleman friend?'"

"No, I—"

She patted my hand. "He's ever so handsome and quite masterful." She gave a dreamy sigh, smiling up at the ceiling. Then her eyes drifted downward. "But here I am, gibbering like a schoolgirl whilst you have more practical matters to which you must attend. I saw you had an unfortunate collision with Beale."

"Yes, but I'll wait in the queue – it won't be long now," I said, though five people stood in front of me, and the queue hadn't moved since I'd arrived.

"Follow me," she whispered with a girlish air. Without waiting for me, she hurried down the corridor and turned the knob on an enormous oak door. I scurried behind, as if someone might catch me breaking the rules.

"Bother. It's locked." She sighed. "But of course it is, you nitwit, you put it in the drawer."

I was about to protest that though I had many faults, being a nitwit was certainly not among them. But I soon realised Lady Charlesworth had been mumbling to herself as she pulled open a small drawer on an end table, removing a large brass key from underneath the flowered paper lining the drawer.

"We keep it locked to repel possible marauders," she giggled. "Though I wouldn't mind a few of those young marauders wandering into my bedroom." She paused. "Do lock up after you've finished, dear." She pressed the warm key into my hand.

After a satisfactory visit to the smallest room, I hurried to the end table, grasping the key in my hand. I nearly tripped over a stack of sheet music and a saxophone case as I made my not-so-graceful exit.

Then I heard the screams coming from down the corridor. And they were most certainly not screams of joy.

5

I scrutinised the scrunched forehead and disbelieving, fixed eyes. Eyes that were trained on Pixley's shoes, as if seeking his help. It wouldn't take a doctor to realise these eyes would never stare again. Rex Camden lay sprawled on the floor, arms akimbo, his fingers just brushing his beloved saxophone. His pale face had turned an angry red, almost as if he'd been sunburnt, and his lips looked dry and cracked.

Amidst the gurgle of high-pitched cries, Pixley grabbed me by the elbows, pressing me into a corner of the drawing room, the same place Nigel had knocked over his drink. Gasping for breath, I plopped down into a chair and surveyed the scene. The odour from the sweating, heaving bodies hadn't bothered me before, but now it felt like I was inhaling thick London fog. Pixley's breaths also came short and fast.

I jumped up, dashed to the window, and flung open the sash. The cool, misting rain fell on my face. Pixley squeezed next to me and drew in deep breaths. "Dreadful. Just dreadful. One moment, we were all dancing, and then the next, I heard a crash followed by a thud. Rex just lay there on the floor. The only thing that had changed was him. Everything else looked exactly the same."

Nodding, I gazed numbly at Ruby, whose head was bent in consultation with Lady Charlesworth. Ruby's calm, direct gestures soon soothed our host, though her hands still trembled. Hattie had buried her face into the folds of Vincent Avery's dinner jacket, whilst Nigel and Ruth both gaped at the body. The drummer, a young man with limp hair the colour of ditch-water, looked dazedly over the tiny round spectacles slowly sliding down his nose. Edith and Beale stood whispering with to each other near the large wooden screen. But someone was missing.

"Did you see Giles Lechmere-Slade, Pixley?" I asked.

"Who? What?" he queried absently.

"You know, the older chap with the quickstep."

The corner of Pixley's mouth lifted, reanimating his normally mobile face. "Ah yes, your new boyfriend. No, the last I saw of him, he was swearing like a Cornish smuggler. That Nigel character trod on his toes whilst he was trying to teach him the tango."

He sighed. "Let's find out what happened, shall we?" Pixley patted my hand, but I made no move from my comfortable seat near the window. "Red, where's your curiosity?"

"It's vanished right out of that window," I retorted, though I was fighting a losing battle against both Pixley and the persistently inquisitive voice in my head.

We sailed across the room. Most guests had dispersed and were milling about elsewhere, away from the ghastly corpse. Ruby, however, made straight for Rex's lifeless body as soon as she had calmed Lady Charlesworth.

"I say," whined the drummer in a thin, reedy voice, "Shouldn't you leave him alone until the police arrive?"

Ruby stayed leaning over Rex. I stepped forward, though

well away from the body. "Ruby won't touch anything – she's been around bodies before," I said.

Pixley coughed. "What she means is that Ruby has had experience with, well, corpses, dash it."

The drummer crossed his arms, frowning, and still gripping his drumsticks in one hand. "I still think she ought to move away from Rex."

"You always were keen on running the show, you little runt," spat out Vincent with sudden vitriol. His face contorted, much like that of the corpse on the floor. Vincent leaned over the drummer, hand propping him against the wall. "It was probably you who knocked him off, wasn't it, Silas? I heard you two arguing last night, you know, right after the show."

"You're lying," sniffed Silas, who looked straight ahead, persistently avoiding Vincent's eye. "You must have misunderstood."

"Are you calling me a liar?"

Silas leapt up and threw his rather insignificant weight against Vincent. His stubby fingers encircled Vincent's throat. "Y–y–you know perfectly well we weren't arguing. You're just jealous of everything Rex had."

Until this moment, Vincent had remained motionless, only his green eyes flashing with anger. He moved his arm upward in a swift motion and then suddenly flipped Silas head over heels until he landed with a crash on the floor, only feet away from Rex's body. Silas scrambled up and looked in three directions at once, as if searching for something. In the tussle, his spectacles had slid to the floor, so he was now bobbing and weaving about, throwing ineffectual punches in all directions.

Then he landed a punch on poor Edith's nose. Blood gushed onto her beautiful white satin gown as she fell backwards, gasping for air.

"Darling!" cried Vincent, who rushed to her side, proffering his handkerchief. This time, it was Hattie's turn to throw daggers in Edith's direction.

Ruth Croscombe stamped her foot. "Enough! Stop behaving like children. Can't you see a man has been murdered?"

"Murdered?" Hattie gave out a sharp little cry.

"Surely he had a fit," protested Lady Charlesworth, a crowd now gathering around her with a general murmur of approval.

"He did have a dicky heart," said Silas.

Ruby straightened and smoothed her gown. "Mrs Croscombe is quite right. Someone has murdered Rex Camden."

6

Chief Inspector Radford gazed over the red spectacles perched halfway down his nose. "What did you say your name was?"

"Ruby Dove, Chief Inspector. Miss Ruby Betto Dove, to be precise."

"Thank you, Miss Dove. We value precision at the Yard." He removed his spectacles from his cadaverous face and waved them at Pixley and me. "And who might you two be?"

His voice recalled one of my older Oxford tutors, who spoke with the most terrific broad A's. Every sentence sounded like both a royal condemnation and a declaration.

"I'm Fina Aubrey-Havelock, and this is my friend Pixley Hayford," I said.

"Hayford... Hayford. Now, where have I heard that name?"

Pixley made a discreet cough. "I fancy you've read my latest in the *Daily Correspondent*, Chief. The piece on Italy's aggression against Ethiopia?"

He shook his greying head. "I didn't read that piece. But you're a journalist. Well, well. Certainly don't look the part, but we'll need to keep you right out of this case."

I squeezed Pixley's hand to keep him from talking. It almost worked.

"But Chief—"

He held up a hand. "Chief Inspector, Mr Hayford."

"I—"

"Please, Mr Hayford. I must attend to these guests and this murder investigation, if it is indeed a murder investigation." He clapped his hands together. "Everyone, please. I'm dreadfully sorry for this intrusion, but I'm keen for everyone who had even the remotest connection to the deceased to remain. If you have not even the merest passing acquaintance with—" he looked down at his notepad "—Mr Rex Camden, then you are free to leave, but please leave your name and address with Constable Jenkins. I must stress that any attempt to pretend that you did not know the deceased will immediately throw suspicion upon yourself."

Guests rushed from the room and into the corridor, soon forming a haphazard queue. Chief Inspector Radford snapped his long fingers. "Roberts, help Jenkins."

With a nod, a helmeted constable padded from the room. Besides the chief inspector, several guests remained, alongside Pixley, Ruby, and me. Ruth Croscombe hovered around Nigel, who was chewing placidly on yet another sandwich. Giles Lechmere-Slade stroked his moustache and sipped from a glass of port. Beale stood with his hands behind his back, near Lady Charlesworth. She was fidgeting with her necklace. Having retrieved his spectacles, Silas Marsh sat on his drummer's stool, arms crossed and one fist grasping his drumsticks. Vincent Avery perched on the arm of a sofa, smoking a cigarette. Their antagonism apparently forgotten or forgiven, Hattie and Edith sat on the sofa, holding hands.

The chief inspector leaned on the piano and squinted at the remaining guests. "I know you've already given your details to my constable, but I wish for each of you to tell me your name, your association with the deceased, and anything that might be relevant to his death. Any detail you might remember. Nothing is too insignificant."

Ever the good mother and member of the community with a capital C, Ruth Croscombe raised her hand. "I'm Mrs Edwin Bantfield Croscombe, but you may call me Ruth," she twittered. "My family has been friends of Lady Charlesworth for many years. Though I did not know poor Rex Camden well, I had met him several times at Lady Charlesworth's events. He was a nice young man, though perhaps a bit arrogant."

"Why do you say that?" snapped Hattie.

"Oh, my dear, I didn't mean to speak ill of the dead. It's just that the young man always forgot my name," said Ruth.

Hattie gave a tiny, unlovely snort.

Chief Inspector Radford cleared his throat. "Yes, well, thank you, Mrs Croscombe. Did you notice anything in particular this evening that might be relevant?"

Ruth cocked her head. "The lights went out, though I cannot remember when."

"Ten o'clock," said Pixley.

"Thank you, Mr Hayford," said Radford. "Any idea what might have caused the power cut?"

Beale coughed discreetly. "It was pouring rain, and we had several electrical appliances on in the flat. Sometimes that causes the lights to go out."

"Where is the fuse box located?" asked Radford.

"In the main hall, sir, near the front door. You'll see it clearly marked if you go towards the door. That's how I remedied the situation."

"I see. Anything else?" Radford asked, turning back to Ruth.

"Well, I did see Miss Aubrey-Havelock, I believe it is," she said pointing to me, "collide with Beale and a glass of orange juice. That was just before Dizzy Blighty started playing." She scratched her forehead. "I cannot quite recall what happened after the collision, but I do remember the next time I looked, I saw the orange juice sitting on the piano."

The chief inspector scribbled with furious intensity on a notepad. I simply couldn't believe he was taking this all down, but I surmised his constables had to attend to the guests near the door. He lifted his head. "Ah, Miss Aubrey-Havelock, would you care to explain?"

"As Mrs Croscombe said, I collided with Beale."

"And why was that? Why were you in such a hurry?"

"The pretty young thing was embarrassed," growled Giles from the corner.

"Look here," I said, rising from my seat.

"Yes, dash it, sir," said Pixley. "I won't have you insulting my friend."

Ruby held a finger in the air. "If I might explain, Chief Inspector? I was also involved in this incident, so I might as well narrate." She flashed an almost imperceptible glare at Giles. "Miss Aubrey-Havelock and Mr Lechmere-Slade had just finished entertaining us all with a most magnificent tango. Knowing my friend well, it was unsurprising that she rushed off to repair her make-up – the tango was quite a strenuous effort, of course, and a lady must always look her best."

I suppressed a giggle. Ruby knew I would never believe such rot. But the chief inspector was nodding thoughtfully.

"In any case, she ran headlong into Beale here, who was carrying a tray with an orange juice for Vincent," she said, gesturing to the piano player. "As Beale needed to clean up the floor, and Fina her gown, I said I'd put the orange juice on the piano, which I did."

Vincent took a long drag on his cigarette. "Before you ask, Chief Inspector, I did request the orange juice from Beale. The juice is a bit of a ritual for us. I'm usually the one to order it since my mouth isn't engaged with an instrument. It's also easier to put a glass on a piano than trying to find a place near the drums or saxophone. The orange juice habit developed because our trio has a strict rule about staying sober during our performances."

"But certainly not after," said a mulish Silas.

Ignoring his bandmate, Vincent continued. "It's critical, or I ought to say it was critical, for Rex to stay away from alcohol. He's the only one of the three of us who cannot afford to have a dry or irritated throat."

"So you're saying he would have drunk the orange juice, even though you requested it?" asked Chief Inspector Radford.

"Possibly. I must admit, I didn't notice if he did. But my head is always focused on the piano, so I might not have seen it."

Silas held up a drumstick. "Ah, Chief Inspector. I saw Rex take a swig of the juice soon after Miss Dove deposited it on the piano. After that, he took another. I don't think he drank any more after that because it was almost empty."

"And you didn't drink any, Mr Avery?"

Vincent licked his lips. "I was simply too busy. Besides, I usually become thirsty only after the first few songs. But by that time, well, poor Rex had…"

"Quite," said the chief inspector. "I've arranged for the glass to be analysed." He paused, looking intently at Silas and Vincent. "Now, how many people knew about your orange juice habit? I assume it was just your trio?"

"I'm afraid not," said Lady Charlesworth. "The orange juice became somewhat of an institution with Dizzy Blighty. Anyone who'd ever seen them perform more than once might have remembered it."

"Which is everyone in this room," said the chief inspector,

almost to himself. "Please raise your hand if you haven't seen them perform before."

Only Ruby, Pixley, and I raised our hands.

Silas stood up. "Look here, Chief Inspector," he said. "Rex had a dicky heart. What's all this nonsense about orange juice and a glass analysis?"

"When a healthy young man ups and dies like this, we need to take every precaution," said Radford. "And I'm a careful man."

Ruby gave a little cough. "Pardon me, Chief Inspector, but I agree with your assessment. I must admit that I sniffed the glass very soon after Rex died."

7

"Miss Dove..."

She held up her hands in a gesture of surrender. "But I promise you I touched nothing. I just leaned over the glass and smelt bitter almonds. I'm among one of the lucky or the unlucky ones, depending on how you look at it, who can smell cyanide."

"Great Scott," breathed Pixley.

"Why did you sniff the glass, Miss Dove?" asked Radford.

Ruby shrugged. "I'm reading chemistry, not medicine, so I immediately wondered what could have produced his death from a chemical perspective, rather than, say, a heart attack. I'd also delivered the orange juice myself, so my attention was drawn to it immediately."

Ruth raised her hand. "I know nothing of chemistry or medicine, but I also thought he was murdered."

"Please continue, Mrs Croscombe," said Radford, cocking his head to the side as if he were entertaining a small child's fancies.

"Well, it wasn't natural, how his body lay on the ground."

"If he'd died of a heart attack, he might have looked much the same," responded Silas.

Ruth's head moved in a circle, scanning the room without focusing on any one object. "Ye-es, that's true, young man. Perhaps it was that. Just what I did right now."

"What was that, Mrs Croscombe?" asked Radford through his teeth.

"Do you mean his eyes were wandering?" I asked.

"Yes, Miss Aubrey-Havelock! That's it." Ruth's eyes gleamed. "I couldn't put a finger on it, but there was something odd about his performance. I'd watched him a few times before, and he either had his eyes closed or fixed on something. This time, his eyes were darting about the room."

"In a furtive manner?" asked Radford.

She put a finger to her lips. "Perhaps. But more as if he were scared of someone or something."

The chief inspector straightened. He was listening intently now. "What was he afraid of? At whom was he looking?"

"That's just it, Chief Inspector," she said. "He wasn't looking anywhere in particular, but his face definitely looked frightened rather than furtive or even belligerent."

Radford finished scribbling and looked up. "Did anyone else notice this behaviour?"

No one responded.

Then Pixley offered, "Fina would have noticed, but she was in Lady Charlesworth's private rooms. But I didn't notice anything in particular myself."

"Does this mean Rexy was poisoned?" said Hattie with wide eyes.

"We must examine all the possibilities, Miss, ah ... perhaps you'll tell me your name and how you knew the deceased?"

"Hattie El Nadi," she said. "Rexy and I met at a party a year ago." She looked at Edith.

Edith tucked a strand of loose hair over her ear. "Precisely eleven months ago." She gave Radford a wan smile. "I'm Edith Lin, friend of Hattie's, and fiancée to Vincent. I'm also Lady Charlesworth's niece. Nigel Shrimpton is my cousin," she said, glancing at him.

"I see, Miss Lin. How can you be so certain of the date you met Mr Camden?"

"The annual Caterpillar Ball is held then – a rather ridiculous name for such an event, but memorable. Hattie and I attended and that's where we met Rex and Vincent." She fingered the hem of her sleeve. "As for what I noticed this evening, I can confirm the lights went out around ten o'clock, and there was a glass of orange juice on the piano, but that is all."

Hattie patted Edith's hand. "I have nothing to add."

As the chief inspector continued his round of questioning, I fixated on that simple gesture. Hattie patting Edith's hand. Though intimate, it seemed out of place. Was it a warning to Edith?

"After I finished my dancing lesson with Mr Lechmere-Slade," Nigel droned, "I did spot Rex sipping that glass of orange juice."

"What time was that?" Radford looked from Nigel to Giles.

Giles puffed out his cheeks, his moustache twitching as he let out the air. "Must have been close on eleven. I remember looking at my watch and considering whether it was time to toddle off to Bedfordshire. Not the young man I once was."

"If the orange juice contained cyanide," said Ruby, "that could have been the fatal sip." She turned to Silas and Vincent. "Do you know what he ate for supper?"

Silas gave us a crooked grin. "As you'll discover, Rex was a fastidious man. A man of habit. He always fasted the day of the performance. The orange juice was his break-fast, as you might say."

"He didn't eat for the whole day?" I asked in an incredulous tone. "Didn't he become weak?"

"Rex said it made him feel clean," said Vincent.

"Ye-es." Redford scratched his chin. "Now, to move on. Mr Shrimpton says he knew Mr Camden through rugby friends, and Mr Lechmere-Slade met Mr Camden through his association with Lady Charlesworth."

He turned to her. "I understand you're a patron of Mr Camden and his trio. What does that mean, precisely?"

Lady Charlesworth drew herself up. "Precisely the conventional meaning of the phrase – I offer them funds, arrange events for them, and attend their performances."

Vincent held up a glass in a toast. "Yes, it's been jolly decent of you, Lady C. We're awfully grateful, aren't we, Silas?"

Grudgingly, Silas nodded. Grudgingly since he apparently loathed agreeing with anything Vincent said.

"And you, Mr Avery and Mr Marsh. When did you first meet the deceased?"

"Silas and I were toiling away in a rather large band that played dreary nightclub acts. When I say 'nightclub', I mean rather something resembling the music-hall stage. Dreadful. We were certainly never paid. I came across Rex through my stepfather, Professor Wharton, who was held up by disagreeable customs chaps at the airport this evening. Rex was his assistant. We became quite chummy once we discovered our mutual love of music. I brought Silas to meet him, and the rest, shall we say, was history."

"Thank you, Mr Avery. Now we come to the critical question. Who among you could have slipped cyanide into Mr Camden's glass? Or rather, the glass meant for Mr Vincent Avery?"

Sharp protests arose from the crowd.

Chief Inspector Radford clapped his hands rather theatrically, but it did the trick. "It looks as though Mr Rex Camden might not have been the intended victim. Regardless of whether this proves to be the case, we must be clear about everyone's positions."

"Are you suggesting a reconstruction?" asked Lady Charlesworth.

"We must be certain of everyone's location at the critical moment. I'm most keen for everyone to move into their position just after Mr Lechmere-Slade and Miss Aubrey-Havelock's tango performance." He peered over his spectacles. "Now," he said simply.

Guests scurried about trying to find the right position, like awkward schoolchildren searching for a seat after their lesson had begun.

Ruby and I had the best view. From my vantage point, I spotted Edith in the queue for the toilet; Beale walking towards me, hand held upright with an empty tray signifying the glass of orange juice; and Ruby standing behind me in the archway. Silas perched on his stool to my right, and Vincent sat with his back to me at the piano, just out of reach of Silas. Rex would have stood in between them.

I craned my neck and spotted Lady Charlesworth a few steps away from Ruby, standing next to Giles, who was seated on the sofa. Nigel stood near the fireplace – presumably near his stash of sandwiches. Pixley hovered near the kitchen and behind him was Hattie.

"Where's Ruth – I mean, Mrs Croscombe?" I asked.

"In here!" Her head popped out of the kitchen. "I thought I'd have a start on the dishes. Force of habit, I'm afraid."

"Right," said Radford, sliding behind me into the corridor leading to the toilet and kitchen. "Everyone is in their correct positions?"

"I can confirm everything looks accurate from my point of view," said Ruby. I lifted my chin in agreement.

"Mr Hayford and Hattie are in the correct positions," said Edith.

"What about Mrs Croscombe?" called Radford. "Can anyone confirm her position in the kitchen?"

Everyone in the corridor shook their heads. "I'm afraid I didn't see her," said Pixley, "But she could have been there – I didn't have a reason to pop into the kitchen."

Beale held a finger to his lips. "I didn't see her, either, Chief Inspector, but I did see her afterwards when I went to retrieve a tea towel to clear up the accident with the orange juice."

Radford rubbed his hands together. "Grand. We've eliminated a few suspects."

"How so?" asked Giles.

"Mr Pixley Hayford, Miss Edith Lin, Mrs Ruth Croscombe, and Miss Hattie El Nadi are all in the clear. Once Beale poured the orange juice – assuming the orange juice jug wasn't contaminated, and my men have already sent it to the lab – those four couldn't have tampered with it."

"Unless Beale himself was in cahoots with one of us," put in Pixley for good measure.

Beale glared at Pixley. "Sir, if I may defend myself, I—"

The chief inspector held up a hand. "No need, Beale. We're just exploring possibilities at this point."

Silas's voice cracked behind me. "Chief Inspector, you must also remove me from your suspect list. As you can see from my position on this stool, I couldn't possibly have reached over and 'tampered', as you say, with the juice."

"You could have risen from the stool," I said.

"He's right," said Vincent. "We played two songs before Rex died, and I would have noticed if Silas had come towards the piano. Besides, he never leaves his seat until our set is over."

"Again, assuming that you two are not colluding with one another, your story lets Mr Marsh off the proverbial hook."

Radford paused. "And whilst it does mean we still have six suspects in total, I'm afraid you're the front runner, Mr Vincent Avery."

8

"Would you answer the door, Feens?" called Ruby from her kitchen. "Pixley's knee-deep in porridge, and I've created a terrific mess with the coffee on the stove."

"Right-o." I hurried from the spare room in Ruby's flat, the peaceful spell of the morning broken. I cinched my dressing gown tighter, anticipating it might be the police at the front door.

Vincent Avery stood on the landing, leaning against the doorframe. Whether it was a casual stance or a position of exhaustion, I couldn't tell, though the tell-tale sunken eyes and dried lips provided a clue.

His eyes widened. "Sorry to barge in on you, but is this Ruby Dove's flat?"

"Oh yes, quite. I'm staying here for a while, and Pixley slept on the sofa." I looked at my watch. "It's been only a few hours since we last saw you. Please come in."

"Who is it, Feens?" called Ruby.

Then she popped her head around the doorframe. "Ah, Mr Camden. I expected you. Please do make yourself at home. I believe we have enough breakfast for you as well."

She disappeared into the kitchen. Pixley's humming drifted down the hall, a pleasant sound complementing the scraping of crockery and a whistling teakettle.

Vincent removed his hat and followed me into the sitting room. "Why did Miss Dove expect me?"

I shrugged. "You'll find out soon enough. She's a genius."

"I see," he said, plopping onto a chair that fitted his beanpole frame. His eyebrows wrinkled as he stared at the wall. "Beautiful painting – is it the Caribbean? I miss it sometimes."

"It's St Kitts, where Ruby's family is from. Were you born in the Caribbean?"

"Born in London, but my stepfather still lives in Trinidad."

"Ah yes, hence the reason he couldn't join us last night."

"Well, yes. Though he hasn't had trouble at the border in the past. I fancy it must be his scholarship – he's becoming more political and cantankerous in his dotage."

Pixley toddled into the room. "Hullo, Mr Avery. What brings you to Ruby's flat this morning?" He wiped his hand on his blue apron before offering it for a handshake.

Vincent opened his mouth but Pixley answered his own question. "This murder business. Well, you've come to the right place."

"I certainly hope so, Mr Hayford."

"May we dispense with the formalities?" I asked. "I'm Fina, and this is Pixley."

Vincent chuckled. "Right you are, Fina. Please call me Vince. And I'm terribly glad I've come to the right place. I'm at my absolute wits' end with the police."

Ruby appeared, holding a tray laden with tea, toast, jams, fruit, porridge, and coffee. I jumped up and helped her lay the table, swiping a piece of toast as I did so.

"Chief Inspector Radford seems a bright bloke." Pixley put a foot on a stool and pulled up a trouser leg. His thinking pose. "Is he putting the squeeze on? Seems unlikely, given the fact they didn't find anything when they searched us all last night."

Ruby's discovery of the cyanide had prompted the chief inspector to search everyone, but no obvious signs of cyanide or any other poison had surfaced.

Vince put his trilby on his knee and crossed his arms. "He may or may not be the sharpest knife in the drawer for all I care, but he has it in for me, that's certain. He even said this morning that 'an arrest may be imminent'."

Ruby waved us towards the table, and we all took a seat. "What else did the chief inspector tell you?" she asked. "Has he heard anything about the cyanide?"

"They haven't finished the post-mortem yet, but the orange juice glass contained cyanide. No cyanide in the jug, though."

"Was the poison meant for you?" I asked.

He set down his teacup. "I cannot see why anyone would want to kill either of us." Without warning, he slammed his fist on the table, jiggling the marmalade and dislodging toast from its silver rack.

Pixley gave me a furtive glance whilst he dunked toast in his runny egg. Ruby pursed her lips and then opened them. "Let me be direct, Vince. You have a temper, and I advise you to keep it in check, at least with us and in the presence of the police."

"Sorry." He peered into his porridge.

"Now." Ruby dipped a knife into the raspberry jam. "Tell us about your relationship with Rex, Edith, and Hattie."

He turned his spoon about in the gelatinous mixture. "I'm engaged to Edith. She's jealous of Hattie, but that has nothing to do with me. Hattie has her hands all over any halfway attractive male she can find."

Pixley choked on his tea.

"Present company included, of course," laughed Vince.

"I saw her eyeing you across the room, Pixley," put in Ruby.

"As I said, she makes a play for chaps, and their girlfriends are jealous," Vince went on. "Edith doesn't suffer fools, so she has been rather sulky whenever the three of us are together."

"And where does Rex come in?" I asked. "Hattie referred to him as 'Rexy' – did it mean anything?"

"I doubt it. It's just her way. I know she seems flighty, but she's rather shrewd – if self-centred. She'd flirt with Rex in front of me, hoping it would make me jealous or pay more attention to her, which had the added benefit of making Edith cross."

"Why are they friends?" asked Pixley. "If looks could ki—" He stopped himself by draining a cup of coffee.

"They've been friends since childhood, and Hattie has known Lady Charlesworth that long as well. The three of them often come to our shows together."

"El Nadi rings a bell." Pixley snapped his fingers. "A few years ago, wasn't Lotfi El Nadi the first African and Arab woman to become a pilot? I'm sure it's quite a common Arabic name, but still, that's why I remembered it."

"Believe it or not, they're actually cousins. The two sides of the family are quite different – Hattie was raised in London, not Cairo, so she barely knows her cousin. But she's enormously proud. Hattie takes after Lotfi in a way: absolutely determined to get what she wants. Despite her surface appearance, she takes her painting very seriously."

He scraped the bottom of his porridge bowl and winked at Ruby. "Compliments to the chef."

"It's Pixley's speciality," said Ruby. "But to return to our theme. Were the four of you under any particular strain?"

"The blasted competition."

"Pardon?" asked Pixley. "Is this the jazz competition in Belgium? Scheduled for this New Year's Eve?"

"How do you know these things, Pix?" asked Ruby.

"I am a journalist, dear Ruby. But you know I adore music of all sorts, especially jazz. It's the first of its kind – an international competition."

"Yes...and Dizzy Blighty might have won. I'm not being immodest about that, either. Rex was a talented saxophonist, and we had been practising day and night. So it naturally caused a few short fuses."

"Like your antagonism with Silas?" I asked.

Vince chuckled and tapped his spoon on his teacup. "Silas and I have a love-hate relationship."

"Enough to kill someone over it?" asked Pixley.

"I doubt it. He has what is politely called a 'dyspeptic personality'."

"And he's irritated by your general air of affability," said Ruby.

"Perhaps you're right," said Vince, crunching into his toast. "I hadn't considered it before."

"That makes it even more frustrating," I said. "You not even noticing why he's irritated with you."

He waved a hand. "Advice received, but I still say he's not a killer."

I swallowed my last bite of toast. "What about Ruth Croscombe's observations last night, that Rex's eyes were darting about? Do you think he was afraid of someone in the crowd?"

"I've been ruminating on that all morning," said Vince. "And I can't explain it. If he had appeared angry, well, then it could have been someone in the crowd – some romantic entanglement."

"You mean jealousy?" asked Pixley.

"Something like that." He waved a hand, though declined to elaborate. "But afraid? Rex wasn't afraid of anyone. Except perhaps my stepfather when he was in one of his moods."

"Did Rex have any particular hobbies or passions?" asked Pixley.

"I can't see how it's relevant, but he obviously loved music and had an enormous collection of gramophone records, and he was rather fastidious in general – which isn't a hobby, but it certainly was a passion."

"For example?" asked Pixley.

"Unlike myself, or even Silas, he had strict routines for everything, and valued purity greatly."

"So that's why he'd fast before a performance?" I asked.

"Bingo. His flat was well-ordered, and he supported various causes that you could say were cleansing, I suppose. He drank moderately, and supported some anti-drugs, anti-gambling, and anti-vice measures. He once even gave money to vegetarians!"

I furrowed my brow. "Why vegetarians?"

"He said meat was unclean and unhealthy."

Pixley chomped on a piece of bacon with gusto.

"If you're finished, I have another question." Ruby twisted her teacup. "Was it you who invited me to Lady Charlesworth's flat?"

"I say," said Vince. "How could I have invited you if I hadn't met you before last night?"

"Well, someone invited Ruby," said Pixley.

"In a rather mysterious way," I put in.

Vince banged the table again, then looked sheepish. "Sorry! But it wasn't from a fit of temper this time. I just remembered who might have invited you. Mind if I ring up someone?"

"Is it expensive?" asked Ruby.

He grinned. "Aha, you are clever. No, the person I wish to telephone is in London."

Ruby rose and Vince followed her into the corridor. Though uninvited, Pixley and I trailed in after them.

In the hallway, Vince was clutching the receiver. "Hello, yes, Father? Yes, you heard the dreadful news about last night. I'm glad you weren't there, and those blasted officials let you through at last." Pause. "I'm not surprised the chief inspector rang you up. I'm their prime suspect," he said with a trace of misplaced pride in his voice. "Look here, I want you to speak to Miss Ruby Dove." Pause. "Yes, yes, she's the one."

He handed the receiver to Ruby, and she waved us in closer for a listen.

"It's a pleasure to meet you, even if it is only via our auditory nerves, Miss Dove," said the raspy but grand voice.

"The pleasure is all mine, Professor Wharton. I hope perhaps we can meet soon, maybe once this dreadful business is over. I follow your work, particularly that in biochemical processes," said Ruby.

"Thank you, dear lady. We shall meet soon, I'm quite certain." He cleared his throat. "Now, as to who invited you to Lady Charlesworth's soirée, it was I."

Pixley raised his eyebrows.

Ruby nodded as if the professor were simply giving her the weather report. "I see. Did you hope to relay a message to me, perhaps about Caribbean activities?"

"I see my belief in you is not misplaced. Yes, I had hoped to have a private conversation with you. But that must obviously wait."

"I'm grateful that you've solved at least one mystery," said Ruby. "And perhaps you can assist us in clearing the name of your stepson."

"Anything, anything!" he said. "I would speak to the police myself, but I'm certain it would only exacerbate matters, you understand."

"Quite, quite," she replied, gripping the receiver. "Could any of the guests at Lady Charlesworth's party have known that I might be attending, or more precisely, that you had invited me?"

A long pause ensued, broken only by Professor Wharton wetting his lips. "Lady Charlesworth might have told them all.

She asked me who I wished to invite, so I mentioned your name and explained what a promising chemist and fashion designer you were."

Now it was Ruby's turn to wet her lips. "That's frightfully kind, but how did you know, and why was it relevant?"

He chuckled. "I mentioned the dress design because I knew you were a student on a meagre allowance, and every new client might help you. What better place to find such clients than a swanky soirée hosted by the likes of Lady Charlesworth?"

Pixley goggled at the telephone. I was also impressed by a famous professor giving such careful thought to a student he had never even met.

"I'm speechless, Professor Wharton, touched beyond words," gushed Ruby.

"Please, no need to thank me, especially if it might have some bearing on this crime. Rex Camden was a meticulous research assistant and I for one shall miss him. His death is a tragedy."

9

Once Vince had left us to our own devices, Ruby paced around the square woollen rug in the sitting room. "Something's not right. I cannot place my finger on it, but it's just not right."

"I'll say." Pixley polished his spectacles. "Though Vince has a temper, I'm inclined to believe he was framed or even the intended victim."

"I agree," I said, "but by the look in Ruby's eye, she's perturbed about something else."

"Indeed, I am." She tapped her teeth. "Feens, when you removed the orange juice stains from your gown last night, did you blot the material, or use water and soap?"

"The spots hardly showed on the material, so I dabbed at it half-heartedly, to be honest. I hung the gown to dry in the spare bedroom."

"Well done, Feens!" She clapped her hands. Never had I been praised for my slovenly behaviour, and it was a welcome change.

Without further explanation, she murmured to herself and dashed down the hallway.

Pixley laced his hands together over one knee. "Whilst we're waiting, let's cook up some scheme of our own, shall we? Two, or rather three, can play at this game."

"What did you have in mind?"

He put a finger to his lips. "We must interview the suspects, though I doubt any will make themselves available should we appear on their doorstep."

"Quite right," I said. "Though if we managed to bump into them, for example, they might tell us something of relevance – if we tell them it's for Vince's sake."

"It's worth a try. Or we might be so lucky as to overhear them in a juicy, scandalous conversation," he whispered conspiratorially.

"This isn't a news story, Pix."

"But it is, dear Red. I'll be the first to break it, too, when Ruby cracks the case."

The telephone rang in the hallway.

"Would you answer that?" called Ruby from the nether regions of the flat.

Pixley sprang to his feet. He looked back as he ran into the corridor. "A journalist's reflex," he explained.

I remained on the sofa, listening intently.

"Yes, yes, this is Miss Ruby Dove's residence. Who, may I ask, is speaking?" Pause. "Ah, Lady Charlesworth."

Drat. His voice lowered to an inaudible pitch.

After ringing off, Pixley returned to lean on the doorway, arms crossed. "That was Lady C. She confirmed she had indeed told everyone who was interviewed last night about Ruby, so any of them could have sent the invitation."

I groaned. "Ruby will be delighted with that news."

"But that's not all. I fancy Lady C thinks of herself as an amateur sleuth as well, so she's invited the guests from last night to an event. She's certain they won't decline the invitation because it would seem suspicious to avoid her. After all, she told them she's keen to interview them, so she thinks they cannot say no."

"What kind of event?"

"You'll never guess."

~

"Pix asked me what one wears to a rugby match, and I said it scarcely matters since it's freezing." I watched puffs of my breath vaporize into the air.

Tyres screeched and the smell of burning rubber filled the little red car. "Nearly hit that blasted rabbit," said Pixley, gripping the wheel with his driving gloves.

Ignoring the rabbit, Ruby replied, "And Pixley said plus fours, a yellow argyle jumper, and a cherry-red cap would be the proper outfit."

Pixley pulled down his cap and sighed complacently. "Yes, I thought it was a rather natty choice myself. I've been to plenty of rugger matches before, but those were with the league rather than the union."

"What's the difference?" asked Ruby.

"The league is less posh than the union."

"I remember reading something about that player who couldn't join the Welsh national team a few years ago because of his race," I said.

"Yes, the clever cove left the rugby union and played for the Welsh league team instead," replied Pixley.

"Glad to hear it." Ruby shivered. "Does this mean that we'll be watching from inside since it's a posh union team? Otherwise, we'll freeze!"

Wisps of chimney smoke rose from the farmhouses dotting the rolling green hills of Surrey. We trundled towards Woking, home of Nigel Shrimpton and Ruth Croscombe. The clouds hung low in the sky, foretelling rain or snow. Were those snowflakes falling on the sheep? Of course, snow would be much more welcome and festive than rain.

"It slipped my mind," I said. "But did you find what you were looking for on my gown, Ruby?"

Ruby turned her head. "My experiment on your gown resembles the curious incident of the dog in the nighttime."

"You mean the hound of the Baskervilles?" I asked.

"Yes, the dog that didn't bark in the night," said Ruby.

"Sorry to correct you and all that, but that clue was from Conan Doyle's 'Silver Blaze' short story, not *The Hound of the Baskervilles*," said Pixley.

"I stand corrected by our resident Holmes expert," I laughed. "But I'm rather dense, Ruby – you'll need to spell it out for me."

"The clue is this: your gown contained no traces of cyanide," said Ruby.

"My gown contained no traces of cyanide," I repeated to myself, trying to take in the news. We passed placid sheep chewing grass in a rhythmic motion, contemplating our motorcar. Did sheep contemplate? In any case, I was certain my eyes held the same blank appearance of a vacant brain, or on the contrary, a furiously intellectual pensiveness.

Pixley sucked in his breath. "And your finding means what, precisely?"

"Well, it could mean two things. First, despite Feens' claim that she removed little of the liquid, she might have removed enough to make it untraceable when I conducted a test."

"Or second," I said, "the orange juice glass didn't contain cyanide."

"Precisely. Which means there wasn't any cyanide in the glass until sometime after I set it on the piano."

"Which means Beale is no longer a suspect," I said.

"Unless Ruby did it," chuckled Pixley.

"You're not amusing, Pixley Hayford," said Ruby in her best haughty voice. "Beale probably didn't do it, though he might have slipped over to the glass during the performance, and no one would have thought twice about it." She pushed back her beret and rubbed her forehead. "What I cannot understand is the position of the glass on the piano."

I squeezed my eyes shut, remembering the scene. The shiny upright piano had been standing against a wall, so no one could have popped out into the corridor and then snuck up on the piano from the other side.

Ruby turned around again. "I see you're using your fantastic memory, Feens. Tell us what you remember."

Closing my eyes again, I said, "I see a gleaming upright piano against the wall. The orange juice is on top, standing by itself." I opened my eyes. "The murderer would have had a deuced difficult time leaning over the piano to pop cyanide into that glass."

"You've hit upon it, Feens. If the murderer had to put the cyanide in the glass *after* I set it on the piano, how did they do it? Too risky. Besides, no one saw anyone approaching the piano – or at least they won't admit it."

"Mmm..." Pixley jerked the wheel to the left, presumably to miss another daredevil rabbit in the road. "Are you going to tell that Oxford don-like chief inspector?"

Ruby laughed. "Can you imagine? As much as I wish to clear Vince's name, our findings mean one only thing."

I groaned. "That only Ruby could have killed Rex."

10

Lady Charlesworth's button nose quivered with excitement. "I'm so glad you could join us, dear." She patted me on the hand. Then she reached her arm behind Ruby and Pixley, guiding us into the tea tent. This had been my first rugby match, and whilst the game had more action than cricket, I still couldn't understand the purpose of rolling around in the cold mud. Though for some inexplicable reason, I had to admit a tiny thrill in watching bodies pile up over Nigel Shrimpton.

One thing I did understand was the purpose of tea, and more importantly, scones and teacakes. Wobbling older ladies distributed the delectable iced teacakes and piping hot cups of tea faster than anyone could run on the rugby field. Ruth Croscombe marched around these servers, adjusting plates piled high with scones and rock buns. Giles Lechmere-Slade sat at a table nearby, making desultory conversation with Ruth as she weaved back and forth, inspecting and clearing up the mounting detritus.

"Now, let me explain our campaign," said Lady Charlesworth in hushed tones. "Ruth is arranging the tea tent.

Dear Giles is helping by consuming as many teacakes and cups of tea as possible," she twittered.

I shot an envious eye at Giles as he wiped crumbs from his moustache.

"Did you enlist Beale? I haven't seen him yet," I said.

"He's simply potty about rugby, so he's taking this as his day off. I'm sure you'll see him cheering like mad from the sidelines."

"What ho!" Silas Marsh slapped Pixley on the back. "What ho, Lady Charlesworth, Miss Dove, Miss Aubrey-Havelock. Jolly good time, what?"

Pixley's eyes slewed to the right, in a gesture I knew well. I had to agree. What on earth had possessed Silas? His eyes shone as highly as his slicked back hair.

Edith Lin slipped her arm around Silas. "Silas, dear, would you bring me a tea, please?"

"Tickety-tock!" Silas skipped towards the queue that now snaked outside the tent.

Edith, too, was the picture of good health. Her white cheeks had a high colour and the tightness around her mouth had gone. In fact, the tightness of her whole body had vanished since last night.

"I must speak to you before Silas returns," she whispered. "You were keen on knowing about anything else related to the murder. I didn't want to confide in that dreadful inspector, and I didn't want to upset dear Silas either."

"Do tell us, dear," said Lady Charlesworth. "In detective novels, the girl who knows murderer's identity is but is slow to speak is always killed to keep her quiet!"

"You're quite right," said Edith. "But you promise you won't tell that inspector. Any of you?" She held up a hand, prepared to swear on the Bible.

We all held up our hands.

Edith moved closer. "You cannot tell that inspector because it reflects poorly on Vince."

Well, well. Edith Lin was a regular snake in the grass. I ought to have guessed as much. And why was she all over Silas like a feeding octopus today?

Lady Charlesworth let out a puff of exasperation, prompting Edith to continue. "Another pianist approached Rex recently about starting a new band. This pianist is well known, and it's probable the band could have won the competition they're all preparing for soon – the one in Belgium."

After a low whistle, Pixley said, "Is that enough of a motive to kill Rex?"

"Wouldn't it only guarantee they wouldn't win the competition?" put in Ruby.

"I love Vince, but you've seen his temper. He can become distraught over small matters. Why, just the other day he flew into a rage about his socks being laundered improperly."

Pixley pursed his lips. "Well, I'd have to agree with him there. Nothing like scratchy socks."

Ruby shot him a withering glance. "What about Hattie?" she asked, letting the question hang in the damp, cold air.

"Hattie?" Edith paused, her eyes moving this way and that. Not in a shifty manner, but more like someone trying to figure out what to say next. "Hattie's a positively ancient friend. She was in love with Rex and is frightfully distraught about his death."

Ruby's eyes flickered. I had to agree. Edith was lying, but I didn't know why – out of denial, or from wanting to protect her friend?

Hattie came bouncing up in a red flouncy frock, red felt hat, and a white silk scarf. Looking down at my heavy overcoat, I felt we had come prepared for two entirely different climates.

"Did I hear my name? They're having a bit of a break in the

action, so I thought I'd have a spot of tea. Absolutely ripping game," she said, smashing her fist into her open hand. "One chap was taken to hospital, and another just collapsed on the field!" She twirled and a slip of paper flew from her pocket onto the cold ground.

Pixley picked it up and adjusted his spectacles. "Looks like a betting slip. Are they putting wagers on this game?" His eyes gleamed. Here was a possible story for bloodhound Pix.

"I'll say they are!" cried Hattie in ecstasy. "And Nigel's team is winning! Yet earlier they were only at fifty to one."

Lady Charlesworth clutched her handbag. "Wagers? Betting slips? But it's illegal!"

"Indeed." Pixley scratched his chin and withdrew a small notebook with a tiny pencil.

Lady Charlesworth snatched the notebook from Pixley. "You'll do no such thing, my young friend."

"I'm a journalist, Lady Charlesworth. That's what I do – write news stories."

"You're my guest at this event, and if you write a story, well, I have friends, shall we say? I'm not without influence, young man."

A heavy presence loomed up beside her. "May I be of assistance, scrumpkins?" Giles Lechmere-Slade cracked his knuckles. Not threateningly, given his age, but it was enough to make the point.

Pixley shrugged. "Fifty to one, you say? Is it too late to place a wager?" Ruby and I suppressed a giggle.

"As our American friends say, if you can't beat 'em, join 'em," said Pixley in his best faux Brooklyn accent.

Giles slapped Pixley on the back. "Good man. Right this way. There's someone I want you to meet."

The pair slipped out of the tent, but not before Pixley turned his head and winked.

"Now that it's just us girls," said Ruby, grasping Lady Charlesworth's hands, "you simply must tell me how you prepared such a successful party – apart from the unfortunate ending, of course."

"I had the greatest help in the world," she said, pointing her chin in Ruth Croscombe's direction. "That woman is a born organiser, isn't she, girls?"

"Absolutely marvellous." Hattie swiped a teacake from Edith's plate and sank her teeth into it. My stomach growled. I'd need tea soon to keep up my strength. "She told us all what to do beforehand, didn't she, Edie?"

"Yes, she let each of us do what we do best." Edith held her nose in the air. "I'm also quite handy at organising, so I sorted out the gramophone records."

"I see," said Ruby. "So, were you each responsible for a different room?"

"I took charge of the decorations," said Hattie. "I'm a painter, so I hung a few of my best pieces around the flat."

I suppressed a snide remark. At least it explained how the narcissistic Hattie had been persuaded to help with party preparations.

"Ruth arranged the back areas," said Lady Charlesworth.

"And Beale?" I asked.

"Beale took command of the drinks."

"And what about the music? Who arranged that?"

"Giles did, dear sweet."

"So Ruth, Edith, Hattie, Beale, Giles, and yourself, Lady Charlesworth, were all in the flat before the event?" asked Ruby. "With access to the entire flat, including your quarters, Lady Charlesworth?"

She blinked. "I expect so. Is it important, dear?"

Without answering, Ruby continued, "And the musicians? Did they arrive earlier to leave their instruments?"

"Rex and Silas did," said Hattie. "Rex helped Silas carry his drums, and he left his saxophone. I remember Rex warmed up on his sax – just to make sure it was working properly."

"Vince didn't join them since his piano was already in place, I assume?" asked Ruby.

"Quite right," said Lady Charlesworth. "I believe he also had an appointment."

Cheers erupted from outside. Everyone rushed from the tent, causing no little end of chaos inside. Overturned chairs and crockery became casualties of the stampede. I heard Ruth cursing behind us in language that would have made a sailor blush.

My eyelids stuck together in the open air. Drat. Snow was falling. We'd need to drive home soon if we were to make it without having to stop somewhere. I did my best to be filled with the spirit of the win, as red-and-white-striped men held Nigel high above their heads, parading back and forth, singing an unintelligible tune.

Perhaps I could nip back into the tent for a bite before everyone else returned for refreshments. I hurried as quickly as possible, even though I sank into the mud with every step. Then I heard a chuckle. And then a laugh from behind the tent.

11

I peered behind the flapping canvas and spied a couple in a passionate embrace.

"Oh, Silas!"

"Oh, Edith!"

Not the most original lovers' banter, but it seemed to do the trick, as they returned for seconds. Canoodling seconds, that is.

Though I wasn't surprised by this turn of events, it did rather throw another spanner in the works for Vince. Or did it? In a rage at his fiancée turning her attention to the drummer, he killed the saxophonist? No, that couldn't be it. Though there was also Hattie to consider. Perhaps her apparent affection for Vince was reciprocated…and then, when he discovered that his fiancée no longer cared for him, he could have killed Rex in a jealous rage over Hattie's flirtations with him?

I shook my head, hoping that the motion might clear the cobwebs. When Ruby explained a crime, it was always far less convoluted, even if the story was still rather complex. There must be a simpler explanation, but what could it be?

"Psst, Feens! Over here!" whispered Ruby, as she hurried around the corner of the tent. "I saw Beale exchanging money with a few men after the match. Do you think he's running the betting scheme?"

"Could be. He's certainly shifty enough to do it on the sly." I pulled her towards the tent. "Come with me. I'm famished! Then we can discuss the little scene I just witnessed."

"What scene?"

"Silas and Edith."

"No!"

"I'm afraid so. Look here, there's a pink teacake with my name on it in the tea tent. Come to that, at least three have my name on them."

Pixley rushed towards us, cap pulled down against the wind and snowflakes. "We must dash – the snow is coming down like billy-oh. I'll fetch my motor and we'll be home in no time." He hurried off.

"I'll just snatch a few of those buns on our way," I said. But my stomach tightened as we turned the corner. The teacakes had vanished. And so had the scones and buns.

"Ruth, may I have just one teacake?" I pleaded.

She ran from table to table. "Sorry, Fina! We must dash. Did you hear they forecast a blizzard in an hour? The food is packed up already."

Ruby clicked her tongue. "Don't fuss, Feens. I know how important it is to feed you. Pixley drives like the wind, for better or worse. I'm sure we'll stop at a pub on our way home."

Infamous words.

∽

"Damn and double blast it!" Pixley cursed.

"Shall I roll down the window?" asked Ruby. "I can brush off the snow from the windscreen as you drive."

"I'm completely useless in the back seat," I apologised.

"If you open the window, Ruby, it will help the fogginess, but not the snow – it's absolutely obstreperous weather," said Pixley.

"Excellent word choice, Mr Hayford." "I couldn't help myself. Perhaps we ought to stop at a pub until the snow stops," I suggested.

"And then we can feed Feens," said Ruby.

"Blast your stomach, Red. But you're right, dash it. We ought to pull over and wait out the storm. Lady C said a pub is up ahead. The others we passed were shut."

At the side of the road, a sign featuring an otter holding a pint glass swung in the wind. "Is it the Toddling Otter inn?" I asked.

"Bingo," said Pixley, pulling into the horseshoe drive. A man in a woollen cap was valiantly shovelling snow already rising well past his ankles.

"Mmm... I have visions of plates groaning with food. And pudding! I wonder what they'll have for pudding whilst we sit by the fire?" I rubbed my hands together.

"If I ever need to commit a murder, you'd be first on my list as a hired assassin, Red. All I'd have to do is deprive you of food and then promise you the largest sherry trifle you've ever seen," said Pixley as he opened the car door.

"I'd prefer an upside-down cake. Pineapple."

Ruby snorted with laughter.

The Toddling Otter did indeed have a crackling fire in a large open fireplace, and a few locals scattered at tables in what appeared to be the public bar. Whilst they weren't exactly inhospitable towards us, they weren't overjoyed, either. The conversation became whispers, and a few men in caps ambled into the next room for darts.

"Here's a table near the fire." Ruby removed her gloves and hung her overcoat on an enormous wooden peg. "I'll have a half pint of bitter and a sandwich if they have it."

"Same for me, plus everything else on the menu, please." I hung my coat and sat down on a comfortable bench by the fire, surveying the inclement weather outside. Sheets of flakes pounded the window, and the fire flickered with every ghostly whining whoosh from the chimney.

"Here we are." Pixley put down two half pints and a mug.

"What did you order?"

"Can you believe it? They have mulled wine. Actually, it's called a 'smoking bishop', and it's made of port, red wine, and innumerable spices. Delicious." He lifted one leg and then another over the bench. "This would be even cosier if we knew we were driving home soon."

As if to make the point, the front door flew open, blowing what seemed to be a foot-high snowdrift over the threshold. The man who'd been so nicely attending to the drive stamped his feet and brushed off his woollen cap. "Blowin' a gale out there." He gestured with this thumb behind him, as if there was any doubt as to what he was referring to. "I saw a few headlights through the snow. Don't think anyone will be going anywhere tonight. Better prepare, Millie. Those folks will want a place to stay and a bite to eat."

"They'll want more than a bite to eat, George Taney."

"A woman after your own heart, Red," said Pixley.

The magical Millie, a woman with rosy cheeks and ample acreage, bustled towards us with an enormous plate of sandwiches, chips, cheese, pickle, and more bread for good measure.

"Here you are. That's fish paste, mince, ham, cheese, and our house special."

Pixley adjusted his spectacles. "Does that feature seaweed or clams?"

"Pardon, sir?"

"It's the Toddling Otter pub, Mrs Taney, I thought it would feature what otters eat."

"Oh, go on with you," she said, giggling, with her tea towel held coyly over her face.

As she bustled off to the bar, Ruby said in a low voice, "At least you have one person who finds your jokes to be humorous."

"Someone else needs to eat." He handed Ruby a plate.

"Touché," she said, smiling. She bit into her sandwich with proper gusto.

Pixley leaned his forearm against the table, stabbing a few chips before loading them into his mouth. "I placed a late bet with Beale and won!" He pulled a few stiff banknotes from his jacket pocket and fanned them on the table.

"How did you manage that?" asked Ruby. "The match had already begun."

"Beale has it worked out so that you can also place smaller bets on individual parts of the match until it's almost over. That's what I did – purely for research purposes, you understand."

"Of course," I chuckled, feeling much better after one cheese sandwich washed down with a healthy swish of bitter. "Is he the ringleader? Or is he someone's minion? Perhaps Giles?"

"Not Giles. He seemed as delighted and surprised with the enterprise as a child let loose in a sweet shop. Whether Beale is the brains, it's difficult to say." He looked at me. "Didn't you say Lady C hired him a few months ago? Perhaps he has a dubious background?"

"He's certainly peculiar," said Ruby. "But I had a moment to ask Lady Charlesworth about his references, and she said they were impeccable."

"Letters are easy to alter," said Pixley.

"Absolutely. And he has a sharp mind."

An image flashed in my head, one of Beale lifting that candlestick over my head. "Though perhaps a little, what, erratic? I wouldn't say mad, but eccentric," I said.

"I agree," said Ruby. "The person behind this would need the mind of a president of the Women's Institute."

"You mean a military general," said Pixley.

"I'd prefer my image, but yes, it's the same difference."

The ruthless efficiency of the tea tent sprung to mind. "Such as a Ruth Croscombe?" I asked, hardly able to believe it myself.

"Precisely." Ruby sipped her pint. "She knows Nigel very well, and they travel in the same circles. It seems improbable, but that's just the point. Scotland Yard's Clubs and Vice Unit aren't looking for a respectable mother of two from Woking. They'd be more inclined to suspect, well, almost anyone else."

"My journalist's nose is twitching most vigorously," said Pixley. "But how does it relate to the murder?"

The outside door to the Toddling Otter flew open again. At first, I thought the howling wind was responsible. But then a few snow-covered, shivering figures stumbled over the threshold and into the bar.

"Would you mind dusting yourselves off in the vestibule?" bellowed Millie, though not unkindly, from the bar.

The figures turned around and brushed one another off, first removing their hats. Then the door opened again, and a few more people crowded into the snow-covered vestibule.

"It's our crowd!" exclaimed Pixley. "See? It's Lady C, Beale, and everyone else. I suppose I shouldn't be surprised – the other pubs we passed along the road to London were all closed."

"By the way," I asked, surveying the new arrivals huffing and puffing their way up to the bar, "what ever happened to Vince? Why wasn't he at the match?"

"Lady Charlesworth told me she'd invited him, but the police said he was not allowed to leave the immediate area around his flat. Chief Inspector Radford was awaiting the toxicology report," said Ruby.

"I say! Our good friends have already warmed the seats for

us." Silas held up his hand, as if he were waving to us in a crowded room. The locals pulled their caps down further over their eyes, peering into their pints.

"Good Lord," said Pixley. "Why is he such a frightfully cheery chap?"

I related the story of Silas and Edith kissing behind the tea tent. He whispered, "So the murder is a *crime passionel*. Silas kills Rex because..." He trailed off and scratched his head. "Wait a minute, that doesn't add up."

"Indeed, Mr Hayford," said Ruby sardonically. "But it looks as though we're going to have even more opportunities to observe the fickle human heart." She pointed at the window, where the last glimmer of sunlight under the edge of the clouds lit up the snowflakes with a rose-coloured hue. "Darkness is falling. We'd better ask Millie if she has rooms for the night."

12

A floorboard creaked.

I held my finger to my lips and crouched behind the door. Ruby and Pixley froze, she with a small blue case in her hand, and Pixley with a woman's silk undergarments.

The floorboard creaked again, and the footsteps receded down the stairs.

"That was close," I whispered, coming out from behind the door.

Pixley stuffed the undergarments back into a drawer. "I'm getting too old for this," he sighed.

"Look what I found." Ruby snapped open the blue case, revealing a syringe.

"Perhaps Edith or Hattie has a medical condition," I said.

"Who does it belong to?" asked Pixley.

"It might be Edith's since it's nearer her bed."

"What are you driving at?" asked Pixley. "Heroin? Some other drug?"

"It wouldn't surprise me. Hattie certainly is lively, though she hasn't been moody."

"And Edith was high as a hat this afternoon," I said.

"Ah, but that was because she was high on love," intoned Pixley.

"Did you find anything else?" I asked.

"Just Edith's nursing licence," said Ruby, raising her eyebrow. "Rather suggestive, that."

"You mean she has access to poison? Or that it would explain the syringe?"

"Both, actually."

I slid a drawer back into place. "Do you think we have time to search the other rooms? They'll be finished with dinner soon, though I suspect they may drink into the night."

"Half a mo." Pixley scanned a note. "It's a letter from Rex to Hattie. It says, *Dear Hattie, It's no good. You belong to another. Let's leave well enough alone. Yours, Rex.*" Pixley looked up. "Ah, but to whom does she belong?"

I sighed. "With Hattie, you'd never know. Could be one of a dozen people."

"It adds to her motive for murder. A jealous rage," he said.

"You are a hopeless romantic, Pixley Hayford." Ruby tapped her teeth. "It's peculiar that she's carrying the note with her."

"If she is in love with him, perhaps she cannot bear to part with it. That would speak to her innocence, wouldn't it?" I asked.

Hurried footsteps came from the stairs.

"Quickly!" said Pixley, opening the wardrobe and disappearing inside. Ruby squeezed in behind him, her eyes widening as she pushed and prodded him further into the depths of the wardrobe, trying to make room. But not even the proverbial sardine could squeeze in next to her.

I scanned the room. A window ledge might have worked in fine weather, but not in this snow. The curtains were too short. The bed was too low. And the wardrobe was too full. The toilet was down the corridor.

"Feens," gasped Ruby. "The light!" She pointed to a high-backed chair in the corner of the room. In a flash, I squeezed behind the chair, removed the large, beaded lampshade and placed it over my head.

The door opened and two sets of footsteps came into the room, one light and one heavy. The light footsteps returned to the door and shut it quietly.

"I just had to be alone with you."

It was Hattie.

Kissing and rustling noises followed. Fortunately, they couldn't see me blush from beneath the lampshade.

"We must go, they'll miss us soon."

I caught my breath. It was Beale.

"Edith and Silas are so wrapped up with each other they won't notice, and I doubt anyone else will care," she pouted. "Damn," she said. "I've something in my eye."

"Here, let me look," said Beale. He sighed. "We need light."

My spine turned to ice, but then, in a heaven-sent movement, the overhead light switched on. I exhaled through my nose.

"There, that's better, my sweet," he said.

"Wait," said Hattie. "I just need my jumper. Nigel and Lady Charlesworth have been monopolising the fireplace."

I closed my eyes and held my breath.

～

"SELKIES AND KELPIES!" said Ruby, using my favourite expression. "Thank goodness for Mr Pixley Hayford and his lightning-quick mind." She brushed dust from her sleeves, presumably left over from the wardrobe.

"Do you think they believed you?" I asked, relieved to be plopping down onto my own small bed, even if it were as lumpy as curdled milk.

Pixley put his thumbs in his braces. "What? It's a perfectly plausible story. Ruby and I were experimenting to see how many people could fit into a wardrobe as part of a re-enactment of the crime."

"But there wasn't a wardrobe anywhere near the scene of the crime."

"On the contrary, my dear Feens," said Ruby. "You told me yourself about potential hiding spots in Lady Charlesworth's room, remember?"

"Hiding spots? Perhaps. It's certainly secluded, and you need a key."

"I'm with Red. What on earth are you gibbering about?" Pixley paused. "Sorry. You never gibber, dear Ruby. I meant, along what lines is your brilliant mind running?"

"Just this. We've all been assuming that the murder occurred almost instantaneously, even if the murderer planned it months or even years in advance. Correct?"

Pixley and I nodded.

"What if it didn't occur instantaneously?"

"You mean, what if something other than cyanide killed Rex?"

"Precisely."

An urgent rat-a-tat-tat came at the door. "Ruby? Pixley? Fina? I must speak to you at once," croaked Lady Charlesworth.

I opened the door to find Lady Charlesworth gasping for breath. Her little hat atop her curls was askew, and I detected the distinct smell of cider. Perhaps she was a little tipsy. Nothing to fear.

"You must come! Edith has been ringing Vince's flat. No one is answering."

We all tumbled after her down the stairs, though I wondered what we could do to assist in the matter. None of us had any special knowledge of Vince's habits or friends. He had probably just gone out for a stroll. I shivered. Perhaps not in this weather.

Edith stood over the telephone, grasping the trembling receiver. If this were an act, she was an excellent dramatist. One of the best, I had to say.

She put down the telephone, her long chin quivering. Silas put his arms around her shoulders as the few remaining drinkers from our little party looked on at the dramatic scene.

"I just rang up his mother." Edith pulled up her shawl around her neck. "She said she'd spoken to Vince a few hours ago, and he said he was curled up with a book."

"That doesn't sound like Vince," said Hattie. "Curled up with brandy or a gramophone record, perhaps."

Edith gave Hattie a tired smile. "He always says that to his mother. She disapproves of his lifestyle, so he just says he's staying in with a book."

"Well, this blizzard would surely compel him to stay inside," said Giles.

Edith chewed her thumbnail and contemplated her shoes.

Ruby cleared her throat. "Have you telephoned the chief inspector? He may have news."

Edith looked up, her eyes glassy and narrowed. "I–I–I suppose I was keen to avoid it. What if they've—" She broke off, burying her head in Silas's arms.

"Look here," said Giles, putting on his man-of-the-world act. "I'll ring up Radford. There must be a good explanation."

A few minutes later, after being put through to the chief inspector, Giles put down the receiver. He squeezed Edith's arm. "Be brave, my dear. He's been arrested. Though they found cyanide in the glass, the toxicologist couldn't find any traces of it on his person. But they still suspect foul play."

"On what grounds?" asked Pixley.

"They checked Vince's bank account as well as Rex's

account. They found several irregularities, or rather, patterns. For the past six months, £25 has been withdrawn from Vince's account several times, and the same amounts appeared in Rex's accounts a few days later. Radford suspects Rex was extorting Vince and Vince was tired of being bled dry. So he killed him."

"But that's purely speculative!" said Pixley.

"Perhaps they have something else on young Vince that he doesn't wish to disclose," said Giles.

A gust of wind howled, rattling the windows. Most of the locals had left several hours ago and Millie was cleaning the bar, pretending that she wasn't eavesdropping. A sleepy hound raised her head from the fire and then snuggled her snout underneath her folded legs.

"Perhaps it's best if we all retire," said Ruth. I half expected her to offer a bedtime story to one and all. Nigel certainly looked as if he needed one, sulking in a corner of the bar.

"What's eating him?" I whispered to Pixley.

"He wanted to score more tries, I gather," said Pixley. "Apparently winning wasn't enough."

"Better than being arrested for murder."

"By the way, why are Ruth and Nigel here at all? Don't they live near here?"

"They didn't have a motorcar, so they were tied to everyone else. They don't live far away, but it was snowing too hard when they came across the pub. None of them intended to stay long – just like us."

"Ruth has made a most propitious suggestion," intoned Lady Charlesworth. "Let's all have an early night. I'm certain everything will look better in the morning light."

13

I sipped my hot cocoa and folded my feet underneath me in a comfortable chair, well away from the draughty window. "Thanks for sneaking the cocoa upstairs to our room." I raised my cup in salute.

"You're quite welcome," said Pixley, blowing on his own cocoa. "Where's Ruby?"

"She's bathing down the hall," I said.

"Hope she's locked the door. I shall look both ways before I return to my room."

I shivered. "Something evil is in the air. The Toddling Otter itself has a warm atmosphere, but we've all brought something nefarious along with us."

"A murderer, that's who."

"Do you think Ruby will solve it?"

"She always does," he said.

"What are your theories?"

He sipped his cocoa and gazed out of the window. "Little point in telling you, since I'm sure Ruby already has it taped out, but here it goes. Let's start with the murder itself. On the face of it, only Ruby could have committed the murder, but we know that's not true, and fortunately Radford doesn't have an inkling about it." Then he leaned forward in his chair. "Unless Vince slipped the cyanide in the orange juice after Ruby put it on the piano – which seems improbable – then the murderer poisoned Rex in some other way."

"Such as?"

"Well, it's just coming to me now as we're speaking aloud, but it must have something to do with his saxophone."

"Something on the mouthpiece?"

"Just so. Perhaps someone put poison on his saxophone reeds," he said.

"But it couldn't have been cyanide – the toxicologist would have traced it."

"Maybe it was some other poison?"

"Even I know that there's nothing that acts as fast as cyanide. If it were another poison, then it would have had to have been administered much earlier."

Ruby slipped into the room.

"Was the water cold?" I asked. "That was much too quick for a bath."

"Someone was bathing, so I thought I'd call Chief Inspector Radford instead."

"You are a naughty one, Ruby Dove," said Pixley. "Here, I brought you some cocoa. Drink it before it gets cold."

"Thanks, Pix. It's what I need." She took her cup and sat on the bed, with pillows propped up behind her.

"We've just been discussing poison," I said. "You are miles ahead of us, so tell us what Chief Inspector Radford said."

"I called him on the pretext of telling him about Feens' gown."

Pixley's cup clattered on its saucer. "You did what? You've just implicated yourself!"

"Don't worry, Pix. Whilst Radford may come to that conclusion, he'd be hard-pressed to find any motive, let alone any evidence. Besides, Rex wasn't killed by cyanide, remember?"

"That's scarcely stopped him from arresting Vince," I said.

"Yes, but Vince had a motive, and Radford's still awaiting the final toxicology results. What Edith mentioned were the preliminary results. I expect he'll release Vince after the report confirms the absence of cyanide in the blood."

"So you telephoned him just to incriminate yourself." Pixley sighed.

"No, I phoned to ask if he'd sent the saxophone to the lab for analysis. Although our chief inspector isn't exactly imaginative – or perhaps he's too imaginative in Vince's case – he is careful, as he said when we first met him. He had the saxophone and all the items in the case analysed."

I lifted my cup. "Well done, Pix." I turned to Ruby. "He was just discussing the saxophone."

"Yes, and he was right. They found something on one of the discarded reeds in the case."

Pixley and I hitched our chairs closer.

"As I suspected, they found atropine, also known as belladonna. It takes thirty minutes to an hour to take effect, but it's difficult to trace in a post-mortem, unlike cyanide."

"And it has similar effects?" asked Pixley.

"Precisely. It would explain why Rex was so red, and why his eyes were darting around the room. Atropine can produce hallucinations, often of faces, trees, and snakes."

I shivered. "I'd certainly appear terrified."

"The only difficulty is that the post-mortem hasn't revealed atropine poisoning. That's not unusual, as it's sometimes difficult to detect."

"Well, that's it," said Pixley. "Rex must have warmed up on his saxophone thirty minutes beforehand. That's when he ingested the poison."

Ruby rubbed her eyes. "I haven't worked it out yet, but it seems likely."

"But that means that anyone in the flat beforehand could have poisoned the reed." I sighed. "We'll have to begin again."

Pixley drained his cocoa. "Never fear," he said in an exaggerated French accent, "Ruby's grey cells will have adequate rest and then *poof*, in the morning, she will have narrowed the suspects to one!"

~

THE NEXT MORNING saw a rather haggard and listless Ruby descending to the breakfast table, one groaning under the weight of kidney, steak, bacon, eggs, toast, marmalade, tea, and coffee.

"Slept a treat," exclaimed a bright-eyed Pixley as he shovelled in another forkful of eggs.

"The fire went out in our room," I moaned.

"And our threadbare blankets were certainly inadequate for a blizzard," grumbled Ruby.

"Bad show," Pixley chirped. "The smashing good news is that the blizzard has passed, dear ladies." He pointed at the sparkling beads of water on the windowpanes and blue sky beyond. "We'll be home soon." Then he intoned in a deep voice, poking his fork into the air, "The Lord of Misrule decrees it."

"Blimey, Pix, you are dashed cheerful this morning." I rubbed my eyes. "Has anyone else been down to breakfast?"

"Millie said I was the first. Good thing, too – we can snatch the best of the lot."

The telephone near the bar rang.

Millie bustled in, set down a tray with a steaming teapot, and picked up the receiver. "Toddling Otter...Scotland Yard? Yes, please put him through." Millie smoothed her hair and stood ramrod-straight. "Hello, Chief Inspector? Yes, I'm Mrs Taney, and this is the Toddling Otter inn. How may I help you?"

Pause. "Yes, yes, Miss Dove just came down to breakfast. Shall I fetch her for you?"

Ruby put down her teacup and hurried towards the bar.

"Yes, yes, here she is." Millie handed her the receiver. "Chief Inspector Radford."

"Thank you." Ruby moved as far as the cord would reach towards the end of the bar, and spoke in a low whisper.

Millie's eyebrows rose.

Pixley said, "She's not hiding from you, Millie. She's avoiding any eavesdroppers lurking in the shadows."

The pub landlady nodded, apparently satisfied with this suggestion, and brought us another piping hot pot of tea.

Ruby rang off and whispered something to her. Millie tapped a finger to the side of her nose, in a gesture I imagine she'd been wanting to practise her entire life. Ruby smiled at her and returned to the table.

"Radford confirms what he told me last night. The final reports are in, and nothing new has appeared. Rex did not die of cyanide poisoning, nor a heart attack. At least not a natural heart attack. There are irregularities in the report, which may or may not indicate poisoning. But the toxicologist cannot confirm or deny it was atropine, despite its appearance on one saxophone reed."

"Radford called you this early in the morning to tell you that?" I asked. "Why would he? He doesn't owe you anything."

"He certainly does not. But he thought he'd inform me since he had to ring up the Toddling Otter anyway."

"Why the blue blazes would he need to ring up here?" asked Pixley.

"He's instructed the inn landlords – Millie and George, that is – to ask everyone to remain here. He's arriving in about an hour."

"Selkies and kelpies, but he's already made an arrest!" I said.

"The new atropine evidence forced him to release Vince. It's reopened the field of suspects."

"I'll say." Pixley wiped the corners of his mouth. "It's more than opened. It's like someone has slashed a perfectly functioning sieve."

I covered my face with my hands. "We're not a penny the wiser. We're simply moving backwards."

Ruby's eyes glistened. "Backwards, yes, Feens. You might be right. Yes, I believe you're right."

14

"Well, of all the nerve," said Ruth, tucking a strand of hair into her halo-like arrangement. "I must return home to Timmy and Tommy. Not to mention my husband. The house will have gone to rack and ruin in my absence."

"You've only been absent a few hours," said Hattie.

"Spoken like a woman who's never had children," sniffed Ruth. "They're all utterly dependent on me."

Nigel patted Ruth's arm. "It's probably just a hare-brained scheme by the police."

"Why do you say hare-brained?" asked Pixley.

"Seemed like the right thing to say. I'm never good at saying the right things," said Nigel.

"But you play a dashed good game of rugger," said Silas, looking much the worse for wear than last night.

We all huddled around the fireplace, some shivering despite the unseasonably warm day outside. I looked at each of their faces, running through the possibilities. Whom did I suspect, now that almost everyone was a suspect again? Each was hiding something – but were their secrets enough to commit murder? Illegal gambling, possibly drugs, jealousy, and money were all reasons to murder Rex, but none seemed sufficient, especially to kill him in such a risky way. Nigel's downcast face and Giles's good-natured bonhomie simply revealed a collection of flawed human beings, but they were all human, nonetheless. I had seen them at their most exasperating, but they must have some positive attributes. Lady Charlesworth was a good egg, for example, and even Hattie seemed capable of empathy, given her arm-through-arm embrace of Edith.

Squeaking brakes from outside broke our silent contemplation. Millie wiped her hands on her apron and marched towards the door. "This way, gentlemen," she said. Radford and a few uniformed constables trundled inside, stamping their feet from the snow still on the ground.

The chief inspector gazed at us expectantly. Then he removed his hat and overcoat and gave them to a constable. "Where's Miss Dove?" He adjusted his tie and scanned the room.

Ruby appeared in the doorway, eyes shining. "Over here, Chief Inspector. I was just collecting my thoughts."

"Well, I'm glad you've finished, Miss Dove, as I'm most eager to clear up this matter once and for all."

"Aren't we all, Chief Inspector, aren't we all," said Giles, peering into his teacup. I half expected him to turn it over and tell us what secrets the leaves held for us.

"I'm just so relieved you released Vince," breathed Edith. "Now we can be together at last."

I raised an eyebrow. A bit overdone, especially for someone who had quite cheerfully implicated her fiancé just yesterday.

"I appreciate that, Miss Lin, but I'll kindly ask you all to refrain from making extraneous comments. I have a few more questions, and then we'll all be able to go home. Well, almost all of us."

Shivering, I pulled my scarf upward, almost to my ears. Perhaps the chief inspector was wilier than we thought, and he was laying a trap to ensnare Ruby. *The Affair of the Bitter Marmalade* had just such a plot line. The detective had invited the real killer into the investigation, and then at the last minute, they suddenly found themselves in handcuffs.

But Ruby's shining eyes told me she had solved this murder and was confident in her ability to make a case. She sat down on a bench near the chief inspector and smoothed her skirt.

"Now," said Radford, peering over his red spectacles. "I expect many of you already know we've can confirm Rex Camden did not die of cyanide poisoning, nor of a simple heart attack. Though we did not find traces of atropine in his system, also known as belladonna, it was found on one reed in young Camden's saxophone case. The toxicology report also concludes he used the reed shortly before his death, as it was still damp and had traces of his spittle."

"Wouldn't he have tasted the poison on the reed?" asked Silas.

"It's possible, as atropine has a very bitter taste. I surmise he inserted the reed on the mouthpiece, put it in his mouth, and then immediately flung it into his case. Unfortunately, he would have already ingested the poison."

"How long would it take to kill him, Chief Inspector?" asked Giles.

"The toxicologist estimated around thirty minutes, possibly stretching to an hour. The killer had practically marinated the reed in the ghastly concoction."

"I'm speechless," intoned Lady Charlesworth. "Am I to understand that dear Rex arrived shortly after our power cut, warmed up on his saxophone, ingested the poison, and then, then...died?"

"Correct."

"But then everyone who had access to his saxophone is a suspect, assuming they had a reason to kill Rex," said Beale quietly from the corner. His brooding Heathcliff look had vanished.

The chief inspector's thin, bloodless lips set in a grim line. "Yes, that's why we released Mr Vincent Avery." He paused, glancing at Ruby. "Therefore, we will review everyone's motives and whether they could have physically committed this murder. I've asked Miss Dove to help us on that score, as she has proved most cooperative in providing key evidence."

"*She's* helping you, Chief Inspector?" scoffed Hattie.

"Please, Miss El Nadi. I'll thank you to keep quiet."

"Thank you, Chief Inspector." Ruby remained sitting but scooted to the edge of her chair. "The first key moment was when Silas and Rex left their musical instruments in Lady Charlesworth's flat during party preparations. Lady Charlesworth, Miss Hattie El Nadi, Miss Edith Lin, Beale, Mr Giles Lechmere-Slade, Mrs Ruth Croscombe, and Silas would have all been able to taint one of the saxophone reeds."

In a rare moment of focus, Hattie said, "But I spotted Rex warming up on his saxophone before he left the flat. He wanted to make sure it was working properly."

"Mmm...so the atropine was put on the reeds *after* Silas and Rex left the flat," said Pixley.

"Yes, although Silas could have put poison on the reed since he forgot his gloves and returned to search for them."

Radford's eyes slewed towards Silas. "What about it, Mr Marsh?"

Silas gulped. "Ah, yes, I–I–I did. I had to search the sofa for them, but I did find them."

Ruby waved a dismissive hand. "It's of little importance whether your glove escapade was a ruse, as you could have put atropine on the reed during the party as well. What happened before the party is mostly irrelevant as the only two people not helping with party preparations – Mr Vincent Avery and Mr

Nigel Shrimpton – could have accessed the saxophone in Lady Charlesworth's quarters after the guests arrived at the party." Ruby turned towards Lady Charlesworth. "Could Nigel or Vincent have slipped into your rooms during the party?"

This discussion of her rooms jolted my memory. The key to Lady Charlesworth's rooms had been in the drawer when I had used the toilet right before Rex's death. The key had been quite warm, so presumably someone other than Lady Charlesworth had used it recently.

Lady Charlesworth rubbed her forehead. "Well, yes. Nigel and Vincent both knew about the key, so they could have accessed my rooms any time."

"Particularly when the lights went out," I said.

"Precisely," said Ruby. "The murderer might have seized that chance. Or, they may have switched off the power themselves. We won't know until one of them confesses."

"I say, have I missed anything?" came a voice from the doorway.

15

A broad-chested constable stepped sideways, revealing the tall, gaunt frame of Vince Avery. His hollow cheeks and tremor in his hand betrayed the trials of the past few days, but he still had that engaging smile I'd seen on the fatal night.

"Ah yes, Mr Avery, please join us," said Radford, motioning to a chair on the outskirts of our circle. He turned back to our crowd. "I asked Constable Peters to drive Mr Avery this morning. It seemed important that he be here."

Vince ran his hand through his hair. "I'm just glad to see the end of this."

Edith dashed towards her betrothed in a singularly unconvincing performance. "Vince, thank goodness you're safe!"

Through his tiny spectacles, Silas shot daggers across the room at this lovers' reunion.

Pixley's eyebrows rose in disbelief, mirroring my own feelings. Not only was it unconvincing, but it was an odd choice of words. Why 'safe'? I didn't trust the police an inch when it came to the treatment of prisoners, but Vince seemed perfectly fine.

Ruby cleared her throat. "If I may, Chief Inspector? You

asked me to explain why someone would commit such a ghastly crime."

"If you would, Miss Dove. I must admit you have more information on that score than we do."

Everyone shifted in their seats, adjusting their clothing or taking another sip of their chosen beverage.

"Let's begin with money," said Ruby. "Particularly the illegal exchange of money."

"A betting ring," said Pixley.

Chief Inspector Radford's eyes narrowed. "We're most anxious to arrest anyone connected to a betting ring, Miss Dove."

Ruby held up a warning hand. "Quite so. Which is why I must request a favour."

Radford grumbled, "We don't give *favours* in the police force. You must know that."

"But you'd gladly reduce a charge if someone names or implicates their accomplice in a crime."

He rubbed his chin. "Yes, but this is murder."

"That's why you'll ignore the lesser crimes I'm about to describe." Ruby crossed her arms. "I'm afraid we'll need to strike this bargain if you wish me to continue."

A slow half-grin lit up Pixley's face. I could imagine him thinking what a 'clever devil' Ruby was, and I had to agree. She'd put Radford in an impossible position. If she'd made the request in private, he might have agreed and then disregarded it when it was convenient. But in front of this crowd? And particularly Lady Charlesworth? He'd have to play fair, at least on the surface.

"My request also applies to those involved in these more minor crimes. Such as betting." She turned towards the crowd. "You must stop. If you fail to do so, the police will be keeping a close watch over you—so don't expect a reprieve."

No one nodded, but plenty of people gulped and held their breath in silent assent to Ruby's directive.

"Now, how does this betting ring relate to the murder of Rex Camden? As you may recall, Rex had a strong aversion to gambling and campaigned against it, as he did against other vices. It was all part of his passion for purification. Pixley, Fina, and I learned as much when Vince joined us for breakfast the morning after the murder."

Silas nodded. "It was an odd but understandable fanaticism, since Rex's entire family had unravelled due to gambling debts. It was a tragic house of cards, and Rex had to fend for himself when they were left penniless. I expect that's where his ambition came from. And his dedication to fastidious routines."

"We also know Beale was taking wagers at the rugby match," Ruby continued, "and that Giles had placed bets already. Indeed, Mr Lechmere-Slade might have already been in debt, given what he told Fina about Argentina and the oilfields he'd invested in whilst they danced the tango. The tango itself might have been a distraction from the murder about to occur. Mr Lechmere-Slade might have killed Rex if he saw this betting ring as his salvation."

She paused, turning on Hattie. "Hattie was also an enthusiastic participant, though it seemed probable she was a casual gambler. Lady Charlesworth seemed scandalised about the betting, but I find it too difficult to believe that her sharp mind wouldn't have noticed the book-making going on around her."

Lady Charlesworth sniffed. "Thank you for the back-handed compliment, dear, but I was unaware of these wagers until the day of the rugby match."

"Look here, young lady," said Giles. "Though I was determined to keep Lavinia out of the picture, I became a little carried away during the match." He patted Lady Charlesworth's hand. "Sorry, m'dear."

She reciprocated the gesture and murmured something to the effect of "snoochums".

Giles continued, "And despite what I told Miss Aubrey-Havelock, I am well out of the woods now regarding those unfortunate wild-cat schemes in Argentina."

No doubt due to Lady Charlesworth's generosity, I thought.

Beale ran his hand over his smooth hair. "I assure you, I was simply an intermediary at the rugby match."

"And I didn't know it was illegal!" squeaked Hattie.

"Be that as it may, I also was certain that Nigel knew about the betting, and may have been providing insider knowledge to the ringleader," said Ruby.

"I say, that's going too far. We all know how perfectly muddle-headed I am," said Nigel.

"You're not as addle-pated as you make out," said Pixley. "I've seen a few rugger matches in my time, and no one who's a complete blockhead scores as many tries as that."

I recalled Nigel at the party that first night, in the role of crashing bore. Whilst his stories about his horrid rugger mates rang true, perhaps he'd been playing the role of blockhead a bit too well.

"Yes, I'm sure the temptation to provide inside information was strong. But he'd do well to avoid doing so in the future. And to steer clear from the ringleader, wouldn't he, Mrs Croscombe?"

Ruth fumbled with the catch on her bag, opening and closing it. "I don't know what you mean, Miss Dove." She laughed, but trailed off into a disturbing, awkward silence.

"You are efficiency and organisation personified," said Ruby. "We saw that the night of the party, and you continued your impressive display of organisational campaigns the next day in the tea tent. If I were to place a wager on the most likely candidate for the head of the betting ring, I'd gamble everything on you."

Ruth pursed her lips and narrowed her eyes. "Prove it."

Rather than respond, Ruby turned to Edith, whose hand was squeezing Vince's arm. "Or, it could have been you, Miss Lin. You have the brains and the organisational skills. I recalled seeing you flipping systematically through the gramophone records during the party. It's as plain as a pikestaff that you think three steps ahead. You made that clear when you implicated your beloved."

Vince gently removed Edith's arm. "What did you say, darling?"

"Oh, it was nothing, Vince. Just a joke, just a joke."

Vince said nothing, but he inched away from Edith. "What did she say, Ruby?"

"That you had a temper and could fly into a rage about the smallest matters," replied Ruby. "Such as improperly laundered socks."

Edith spluttered, but Ruby persisted. "Your relationship with your fiancé merely shows us your keen sense of timing and organisation. That's why you were my second choice for the ringleader, out of three possibilities."

"Three?" said Silas. "Who is the third?"

"Lady Charlesworth, of course," said Ruby quietly.

16

Giles rose and stamped a foot. "Now see here, I won't have Lavinia's name bandied about in such a loathsome manner."

"Giles, please, darling." Lady Charlesworth pulled at his sleeve.

He remained standing. "If you were a man, I'd settle this outside."

Pixley and I broke into a fit of giggles. It was wholly inappropriate, but it served to divert attention. We soon quieted down.

"Sorry," said Pixley. "No offence taken, I hope, Mr Lechmere-Slade."

"Thank you, young man."

Ruby cleared her throat. "It is irrelevant whether Lady Charlesworth, Mrs Croscombe, or Miss Lin is the actual ringleader, because it offers each a reason to risk committing murder. That is all we need to know at the moment."

I scanned the room, wondering if everyone else felt as bewildered as I did. Silas was frowning, but the candidates for ringleader position simply looked relieved.

"My apologies for being vague, but all will soon become clear," said Ruby. "Now, as for other reasons people would risk the gallows, various love triangles involved Vince, Silas, Rex, Edith, and Hattie." She turned towards the corner. "Even one included Beale."

"In fact," she said, "these relationships are so complex that I'm not certain if the parties themselves can understand the consequences. Each had a motive to kill Rex from romantic jealousy, though again, it is difficult to say whether it was enough for murder." She paused. "It's also possible that drugs were involved in Rex's murder. But again, I have no concrete evidence of the fact, other than a syringe we found."

I held my breath. Would she reveal where she found it?

Chief Inspector Radford held up a hand. "Miss Dove, it's admirable how you're keen to give certain ne'er-do-wells a second chance, but I must protest as an officer of the law. You cannot shield these people, especially in the case of drugs."

"I quite understand your position, Chief Inspector," replied Ruby, "but let us leave it for now. I suspect those involved are drug users rather than sellers, and I imagine they'll consider seeking medical treatment after this warning."

Edith's mouth opened in obvious horror, whilst Hattie merely drummed her fingers on the tabletop.

Radford frowned. "I've gone along with this unusual performance for long enough, Miss Dove. I've given you much more leeway than you had any right to expect."

What a smug stuffed fish, I thought. Though I was also anxious to discover the murderer.

Ruby smoothed her skirt, unperturbed. "Scarcely anyone here is more eager to conclude these proceedings than I am. In fact, my innocence remains in doubt until I do."

"Pardon – I must have missed something. Did you have a reason to push Rex Avery off this mortal coil?" asked Radford in a fit of literary inspiration.

"Oh no. You misunderstand me. Only two people could have

committed this murder. *Everyone*, except myself and my friends, had a reason to kill Rex. And *everyone* could have dipped Rex's saxophone reed in atropine, bringing about his death soon thereafter. But only two of us could have done it."

∿

ALL HEADS LEANED FORWARD. Complete silence reigned, except for the squeaking of glasses being dried by Millie's tea towel.

"Yes, only Mr Vincent Avery and I could have committed this crime."

Now it was Pixley's turn to protest. "But Ruby, you were so helpful to Vince. You were absolutely certain of his innocence!"

Vince's face had scrunched into an unlovely imitation of a gargoyle adorning an Oxford college. "You filthy, double-crossing bi—"

"That's enough of that, Mr Avery," said Radford in a relaxed but firm voice, signalling to a constable to come stand by the accused. "Everyone, including Mr Avery, must remain silent. You'll have time enough to defend yourself."

Ruby continued, though her voice cracked as she began. "It pains me to speak, especially as I have such an affinity with your stepfather, Vince. He's such an eminent scholar and humanitarian."

Vince said nothing, but crossed his arms and smirked.

"As with many murders, distraction was the critical element. But I was stunned by just how much the proverbial smoke and mirrors had appeared in this case. It seemed nearly any of us could have done it, and what's more, a surprising number of people had a reason to commit such a cold-blooded crime. To make matters worse, everyone had the chance to poison the reed, though we didn't know that at first. Even when we thought cyanide rather than atropine poisoning was the culprit, however, there were still suspects aplenty."

"Yes, yes. We know all this, Miss Dove," said Radford impatiently.

Ignoring him, she pushed forward. "It's so simple when you pause to consider it. First, unless there were two, uncoordinated murderers attempting to poison Rex at nearly the same time, there was only one murderer – and that person used both atropine and cyanide."

"But why?" I asked.

"Precisely, Feens. Why? I soon realised we had a nervous murderer on our hands. In hindsight, this nervousness was justified. It would be an audacious risk to turn out the lights, sneak into the back room, coat a reed with atropine and then hope for the best – or rather, the worst."

"He must have swiped the torch we were looking for when the lights went out," I said.

"Probably. Not only did Vince risk being caught, but the plan itself might have gone pear-shaped. Rex could have removed the poisoned reed before using it, deciding another reed would sound better. If so, then the murderer might be in even more difficulties if Rex used the reed later, even in the murderer's presence. Or simply didn't use it at all and threw it in the rubbish bin."

"So the cyanide was a fallback plan?" asked Pixley.

"Yes, in case the atropine didn't work. Or even worse, if it did work enough to make Rex hallucinate but not die – then Vince would be in dire straits." She paused. "Feens, would you help us set the scene? Remind us of where everything was located that night."

I closed my eyes. "The trio is set up in an alcove in the drawing room. Silas and his drums are along one wall and Vince and his piano are perpendicular along the other wall. Rex is standing between the two but still in front of them. The archway where I had my collision with Beale is to the left of the drums, whilst there is no exit on the other side of the piano."

"Thank you. So Silas could watch both Rex and Vince's movements, but both Rex and Vince needed to look over their shoulder or to the side to see Silas and each other. Vince was the only one of the three with his back to the room and most of the guests, though he could easily glance over his shoulder."

Pixley rubbed his chin. "I see. That means that Silas can watch Vince all the time, and Vince is the only one with his back to the crowd. And that's important because he couldn't see the collision with the orange juice?"

Ruby nodded. "When Fina mentioned something about things being 'backwards', everything fell into place. Vince was the only one in the room – besides those elsewhere in the flat – who couldn't see the collision. We know now how significant that collision proved to be."

"I'm still confused about why Vince used two poisons in the first place," I said.

"If the atropine had worked, and Fina and I hadn't been present, then Vince might have been in the clear. We know Rex had a weak heart and atropine is difficult to trace. The police might have thought it was a tragic but natural heart attack. These things do happen to young people, though it is rare."

Radford chewed on the arm of his spectacles. "It's quite possible, yes. We would have conducted a post-mortem, but as you say, the atropine might not have been detected. Especially as there was no need to test for it specifically."

"Then why use the cyanide at all?" asked Pixley.

"I suspect Vince planned to slip the cyanide into the orange juice when the trio had a longer break between songs. He couldn't put it in before that, however, because it's probable that Silas would have spotted him. Besides, all eyes were on the trio, even during brief breaks between the songs. Vince was waiting for a longer break. Unfortunately for him, Rex died before this longer break occurred."

"Then he panicked?" I asked.

"You could call it panic, or you could call it a quick wit. We may never know whatever prompted it, nor is it vital in identifying Vince as the murderer. It's possible that once he saw Rex lying on the floor, Vince realised the police might suspect something other than a heart attack. In that case, they'd search everyone."

"Which we did," said Radford with a satisfied smirk.

"Vince had to act quickly. He had to dispose of the cyanide, and in such a way that no one – or rather everyone – would be suspected. It was a brilliant act of misdirection, even if it was born of panic. As everyone gathered around the body, he seized his opportunity. Silas, in particular, was focused on the body, so Vince could empty the cyanide powder into the orange juice glass. No one saw him do it."

"But then you sniffed the glass."

"I'm afraid it was force of habit," said Ruby. "As I said the night of the murder, since I'm a chemist and not a doctor, my first inclination is to wonder what caused the reactions I witnessed. I'm unfortunately no stranger to dead bodies, either. When I scanned the room for what he might have swallowed, my eyes naturally fell on the juice glass, especially since I had delivered it myself!" The corners of her eyes crinkled. "Perhaps a bit of unconscious self-preservation was also involved. In any case, I sniffed the glass and smelt cyanide."

"Would you have smelt the cyanide before, when you had delivered the glass – assuming it had been in the glass?" I asked.

"Perhaps. Perhaps not. It was one reason I was prompted to test your gown for the presence of cyanide, Feens."

"So why didn't Vince succeed?" asked Pixley. "He slipped the cyanide in the glass in time to evade the police and to implicate anyone who happened to have wandered by the piano whilst the trio was playing."

"Yes, but not *after* Rex died. There were just a few minutes in which anyone could have used the distraction of Rex's body on the floor to put the cyanide in the glass before I sniffed it. And anyone who'd seen Beale and Fina collide with the orange juice might have realised that their plan wouldn't have worked."

"Because we would have then known the cyanide *couldn't* be in the orange juice *before* Rex died," said Pixley.

"That was the fatal error. If he had slipped the cyanide in the orange juice before Rex died, Silas would have seen him. Therefore, he couldn't be the murderer. But he didn't *see* the collision that established that the orange juice was cyanide-free when I brought it to the piano."

"And this all happened because Vince faced the wall at the piano rather than the room," said Pixley, frowning.

"You're forgetting something, Miss Dove," said Vince.

"Oh yes?" she said, her voice low.

"You're forgetting that someone else could have put the cyanide in the glass – as you said – after Rex died and before you sniffed the glass."

"Who?" asked Radford.

Vince licked his lips. "Well, I didn't want to cause trouble, but it was Silas."

Silas gasped. "You beastly—"

Pixley held up a hand. "I will testify I saw Silas move from his drums immediately to the floor and then stand at the side. He was well away from the piano."

His eyes wild with fear, Vince cried, "It was Hattie!"

"I'm sorry, dear Vince," said Lady Charlesworth. "It pains me to say it, but I had my eye on Hattie and she was nowhere near the piano. She was near the archway."

"It was the lot of you! It was a conspiracy!" Vince jumped up, only to be pulled back down by Edith.

"No, Vince. You attempted the perfect murder, but your plan was too complicated. The more moving parts, the more things could go pear-shaped," said Ruby. "And they did, in the end."

"Indeed," said Radford. "It was almost perfect. But who would have counted on the poison that *didn't* kill Rex implicating you as the murderer?"

"As Ruby said, it's backwards." Pixley glanced at Vince and shook his head. "And I thought you were a decent chap."

17

Pixley crumpled *The Times* on his lap, sending his delicately balanced cap tumbling to the floor. "Jupiter's Teeth! Did you see this?"

I scooped up the cap and placed it at a rakish angle on Pixley's bald head. Such a rakish angle, in fact, that he couldn't see anything.

He tipped it back and thrust the paper into my hands. "Read it! Read it!"

The letterbox rattled in the hallway. "Must be the post," I said, placing the crumpled sheets back on his lap.

"I'll fetch the post!" came Ruby's voice.

The pleasant silence of our morning routine at Ruby's flat had been broken. I had spent a few more days at Ruby's whilst workmen finished whatever they were supposedly doing to my building. Pixley occasionally slept on the sofa since Ruby's flat was closer to his newspaper office as well as the watering holes of journalists.

He rubbed his eyes. "You must read it, Red. Perhaps my late night of carousing made me mix up the words in my head."

"Doubtful," I said, reaching for the paper.

Ruby entered with a stack of letters. She sat down on her favourite chair and poured herself a cup of tea.

"Anything interesting in the post?" I asked.

"I'm more eager to hear about what caused the ruffling of newspapers and cries of confusion from you two."

I had no need to ask Pixley which article had caused such excitement. The newspaper sported a smiling photo of Vince at the piano below the headline 'Vincent Avery Escapes'.

"Selkies and kelpies," I breathed.

"Just so," said Pixley.

"Well, go on," said Ruby. "My tea's getting cold."

I read aloud, "In one of the most daring escapes England has seen in years, Mr Vincent Avery, disguised in a constable's uniform, fled Wandsworth prison yesterday morning. Mr Avery was awaiting trial for the murder of Mr Rex Camden..." I blinked and looked up. "The rest is what we already know."

"The old devil was even cleverer than we thought," said Pixley, rubbing his lips.

Ruby set down her teacup and brushed a speck of something from her skirt.

"You don't seem surprised," I said, handing Ruby the newspaper.

She smiled and waved it away. "No, I'm sure it sounds rather superior to say it – especially after the fact – but I'm not surprised. As Pixley said, he's a clever devil."

Pixley leaned forward, staring at Ruby. "You not only seem unsurprised, but rather unconcerned. Aren't you the queen of injustice? Isn't this an injustice?"

"Mmm..." She suddenly stopped her idle shuffling of the post. "It's a letter from Professor Wharton!"

"Well, at least we know you have the capacity to be surprised by something," chuckled Pixley.

"Now it's my turn to say, 'read it'!" I said, still utterly baffled by Ruby's casual reaction.

Ruby pursed her lips and unfolded the letter. She scanned it, rubbed her forehead, and handed it to me. "I cannot bear to hear it read aloud. Pass it along to Pix when you're finished."

Dear Ruby,

I felt compelled to write you after the police paid me a visit this afternoon regarding Vincent. You will have seen the news in the papers by now.

I wished to write earlier, or even telephone, but the sad truth is words failed me. I've known for some time that my stepson was destined for trouble.

He's most intensely charming but then demonstrates the most wanton callousness I've ever witnessed. He also began to meddle in my affairs, you understand. This behaviour was difficult enough when it was limited to our small family circle, but it had spread beyond to my contacts in various places.

I began to worry about others' safety, not because I thought he would harm them, but rather I was afraid he might disclose information that would lead to someone being harmed. I was prepared to ask my wife to halt his generous monthly allowance, though I didn't have any concrete justification for doing so.

All of this is to indicate that you ought not to reprove yourself for anything involving his conviction, though that seems improbable now, given his escape. Should he attempt to travel to Trinidad, I expect he'll still find it difficult to escape the long arms of colonial law, for better and for worse – though mostly for worse.

Please know that I still hold you and your work in the highest esteem. I hope that we shall meet one day under better circumstances.

Sincerely,

Eldred Wharton

I handed the letter to Pixley and turned to Ruby, who was staring out the window. "What does he mean about 'his affairs'? That part is rather vague," I asked.

"Ah, I believe he means our mutual political activities in the Caribbean. Vince was, or rather still is, a loose cannon. I'm sure he was disclosing all sorts of secret activities that might end up harming people involved."

I drummed my fingers on the chair. "You mean if someone were organising a workers' strike on St Kitts, for example, he might give the names of those involved to someone with power? Then that would lead to their arrest and possible execution for something akin to treason?"

"Absolutely. That's one reason I had few qualms about discussing his crime in front of the police."

Pixley put down the letter. "But he would have surely gone to the gallows with what you found. You've never provided evidence before that would lead to an execution."

"I wasn't about to do so now, either," she said.

"What?" I exclaimed. "But you created an airtight case in front of Radford. Weren't you going to testify at Vince's trial?"

"Yes, but I'd have a bit of a memory lapse, Feens. Just enough to make sure he wouldn't go to the gallows."

"You're a better man than me, Ruby Dove," said Pixley.

"That's because I'm a woman," she chuckled. "But seriously, I know we all agree that execution is abhorrent, and certainly has destroyed so many innocent people."

"But that's not why you oppose it," I said. "You oppose it because you don't believe in an eye for an eye, do you?"

"I do believe in justice, but the state killing on behalf of others, no I do not."

"I agree. I suppose you must be relieved that he escaped," I said.

She cocked her head. "I'm not sure, to be honest, how I feel about it."

"Are you willing to discuss the case a bit more now?" asked Pixley, leaning forward. Ruby had been completely silent about the matter ever since the police had led Vince from the Toddling Otter in handcuffs.

She crossed her legs and laced her fingers over her knee. "Yes, I'm sorry for being so aloof about it all. It was so disturbing, wondering what would happen to Vince. Though even if I had offered everything I remembered at his trial, I still believe the evidence was too circumstantial."

Pixley scratched the back of his head. "You may be right. Even if the jury believed your testimony about Vince being the only one able to slip the cyanide in the glass, it's arguable – though patently ludicrous – that there were two murderers. One using the atropine, and another would-be murderer using the cyanide."

"Indeed," she said. "Well, I expect you're keen to know all about the betting ring to begin with."

Pixley and I nodded.

"I'm nearly certain the person behind it was Lady Charlesworth," she said.

"By Jove." Pixley bounced his fist off the arm of the chair. "I was certain it was Ruth!"

"Me too," I said. "Ruth lived close to Nigel, and they travelled in the same circles. Besides, Ruth seemed bored with her life."

"I agree that poor Ruth seemed rather bored with little

Timmy and Jimmy – or whatever their names were – but Lady Charlesworth is still the more probable candidate. I simply couldn't swallow her story about not knowing about the betting, and she is Nigel's aunt and Beale's employer. She was already involved in what appeared to be a complex patronage relationship with the trio, and she's incredibly sharp and observant."

"She is quite thoughtful and observant," I said, recalling how attentive she'd been after my tango into ignominy and dance with the orange juice. "Do you think she'll stop now that we've notified the police?"

Ruby tapped her teeth. "She'll probably stop this betting scheme, but she'll have her hand in something else illicit soon enough. She, like Ruth, needs plenty of stimulation."

"Talking of stimulation, would you pass me the teapot, Red?"

I absently handed him the teapot and gulped my own tea. "What about the drugs angle and Edith's syringe?"

"Ah, yes. Thank you for reminding me. It's possible some of them take drugs, of course, but I think the syringe was what it appeared to be: simply part of Edith's nursing kit. Though it does suggest Vince may have been able to secure the poison through her."

"You mean she gave it to him?" I spluttered.

"No, I expect Vince cleverly procured it through her without her realising it."

"Yes, yes," said Pixley impatiently. "All very well and good, but what was the real motive for killing Rex?"

"I doubt we'll ever know for certain, but I expect it had been building for some time. As Professor Wharton mentioned in his letter, Vince could turn from charming to ghastly behaviour quite rapidly. What he mentioned at breakfast that day about the jazz competition rang true, especially given his temper. I could tell Vince was one who wouldn't take a perceived injustice lying down."

"You mean he felt slighted?"

"Yes. Rex could have wanted to start his own band, leaving Silas and Vince behind. Vince's ego simply couldn't take such a blow. As for the money that seemed to be transferring accounts, it's entirely possible that was extortion on Rex's part, probably for something Vince had done in his Mr Hyde moments that he wasn't keen to reveal. If these misdeeds came to light, his stepfather might have cut off his allowance."

"Hmm..." I said. "It's almost as if you had a premonition before the murder."

"What premonition?" asked Ruby.

"Remember sitting in the kitchen at Lady Charlesworth's flat? You were staring at a fly and said that Pixley had said something about a stranger that distracted you."

"Ah yes. It wasn't so much about the stranger, but how someone can make one misstep and leap from the category of 'acquaintance' to that of 'stranger'."

"You mean the chap who called me Hairy Pate?" Pixley grimaced.

Ruby laughed. "Yes, that's the one. I was struck by how quickly people can change personalities. I suppose it was a kind of premonition about Vince, but I really had no idea – I hadn't even met him yet!"

"Perhaps," I said mysteriously. "But you know I don't believe in coincidences. Which brings us to the love triangles, or rather love webs. Do they have anything to do with the murder?"

"Again, it's difficult to say, especially since they seem to mostly involve Edith being jealous of Hattie, and Hattie putting it about a bit, as I believe the saying goes."

"You mean between Rex, Vince, and Beale?" asked Pixley.

"Yes, though I couldn't fathom how it would induce Vince to commit murder since he was engaged to Edith. Unless he intended to break it off and wanted Hattie instead, who was currently in love with Rex."

"Seems far-fetched to me," I said. "And if he were jealous of Edith's attention to Silas that occurred after Rex's death anyway, then he should have killed Silas."

"Indeed," said Ruby. "I think the love triangle was actually something entirely different." She lowered her voice, as if someone might overhear us. "Something I wasn't keen to mention at the Toddling Otter. Just like I wasn't keen to implicate Lady Charlesworth directly. Do you remember how Edith and Hattie were throwing daggers at each other all night at the party?"

"Do I ever," said Pixley. "Now there was a case for murder."

"I thought the same until that peculiar scene after Rex's death. Hattie and Edith were sitting on the sofa holding hands. Later, at the Toddling Otter, they sat arm-in-arm. There was a curious intimacy about these gestures. And if I interpreted these gestures correctly, it would also explain Edith's particularly bizarre behaviour, first regarding her lies about Hattie, and second, her lightning romance with Silas."

I blinked.

Pixley snapped his fingers. "You mean they were lovers! Of course, they act like they loathe each other and betray each other. The oldest trick in the book."

"Precisely."

My mouth dropped open. "One moment. Then that letter to Hattie, where Rex said she belonged to another, was actually about *Edith*?"

"Yes, that letter had a particular finality about it that struck me as odd in relation to Hattie. She was so flighty when it came to relationships, but those words about 'belonging to another' were rather permanent." She paused. "Now you understand why

I wasn't keen to discuss the letter and the relationships. All the seemingly casual relationships connected to the pair suddenly made sense. They were smoke and mirrors for the main drama between the two of them. That's why I couldn't clear up the jealousy motives in the presence of everyone else, particularly the police."

Pixley nodded. "Even though homosexuality is a crime among men, and not among women, it would have been deuced difficult for them had you revealed their secret." He poured himself a cup of tea and downed it as if it contained something stronger than caffeine.

Sensing the increasingly dour mood, I set down my tea and wiped crumbs from my skirt. "Well. That's that. Another triumph, Ruby. You successfully solved a murder, avoided endorsing any further use of vile hanging, stopped an illegal betting ring that admittedly was harmless, but did so without harming anyone, and also successfully avoided publicly revealing a secret that would not go unpunished. I'd say things couldn't have turned out better."

I sniffed the air. "What's that smell?"

Pixley leapt up and ran into the kitchen. "I was warming some buns from the corner shop. All part of the season of good cheer." He soon returned with a heaped tray of buns and fresh tea.

"Here's to good friends, hot tea, and the most delicious buns in London," he said.

The End

Continue Ruby and Fina's adventures on the next page with a preview of *Death in Velvet*!

If you enjoyed *Fatal Festivities*, would you leave a splendid review (Australia, Germany, UK, or US)? Ruby and Fina would be ever so grateful. Thank you!

Join my readers' group for updates and goodies!

PREVIEW: DEATH IN VELVET

"May I help you, miss?"

I ignored the question, running my finger against the silky tangerine suit. Though sceptical of the skirt's stitchwork, I admired its design. For good reason, too. I had already seen this copied suit elsewhere.

The rail-thin shopkeeper glared, her severe brown shingle swinging across her pale cheeks. She pursed her lips, hiding the angry carmine slash lining her mouth.

"Thank you," I sighed dreamily, ignoring the tinge of sarcasm in the shopkeeper's voice. "It's a smashing suit, but how much is it?"

Holding up her hands, the shopkeeper swept between me and the tangerine suit, defending it against possible defacement. "Perhaps you'd prefer to peruse the aisles of Woolworths for... something more suitable." She raked her eyes over my serviceable red frock, halting only at my shabby shoes for additional scrutiny.

I shook my head, fighting an urge to wipe her lipstick from her smug face. "I don't wish to purchase the suit, but I am curious about its provenance."

"Provenance?"

"Yes, as in who designed it?"

She sniffed. "All our designs are Madame Mathilde Lafitte's creations. From Paris, of course." She fluttered her arm in a semicircle around the shop, pointing to burgundy, sapphire, and emerald bias-cut silk gowns lining one wall while velvet gowns with daring V-cuts hung on the other.

"Well, I'm frightfully sorry, but that's simply impossible," I said, my shoulders scrunching up in rising anger.

"Are you a designer, then?"

Her query wasn't a question at all. It was a challenge.

"No, but my best friend is, and I'm her seamstress. And I can detect a copy when I see it." I waved the sleeve of the tangerine suit at her. "The colour, cut, and design are all the same."

"Copy?" She arched her over-plucked eyebrows. "I know who you must be. You're one of those tawdry little seamstresses from House of Whats-it. You're trying for a bit of extortion, aren't you?"

I countered by lifting my own less-than-perfectly thin eyebrows. "Extortion?" My face must have been scarlet by now – it certainly felt hotter than Hades. "You're just a toffee-nosed cow, or even worse, someone wanting to join the ranks of toffee-nosed cows. I wouldn't ever stoop so low as to take your money or your poorly plagiarised designs."

A few heads popped out from behind the curtains at the rear of the shop, gasping and giggling.

Grabbing my arm, the woman marched me towards the door. Her cloying sandalwood perfume and firm grip made me struggle, but the shopkeeper's muscles had apparently been toned by accosting customers on a regular basis. To make matters worse, I had an audience now, even if they were only the silly shop assistants peeking through a clothing rack.

"Let me go!" I spat out. "I'll take this story to the newspapers.

They'll be delighted to uncover a fashion scandal and extortion. Extortion of your clientele at these utterly ridiculous prices for copied frocks. And shoddy frocks at that. The stitching is second rate. No, I'm wrong – more like fifth rate."

The shopkeeper let my arm drop, while her mouth did the same. Perhaps it was just my imagination, but people had begun to gather outside the shop. The front bow window made the shop into a fishbowl, so it was scarcely surprising that pedestrians should notice any drama unfolding inside.

Now with an audience both inside and outside, I marched down the stone flag steps, only missing one along the way. A woman with gooseberry eyes goggled, while a man leaned against a lamppost, pretending he was reading a newspaper. Over my shoulder, I saw the shopkeeper dragon fling her head back and stalk off, right past her snickering minions.

Although my mother would undoubtedly have disapproved, I stuck out my tongue at the shop window. Then I strode into the meandering West End crowd, feeling a mixture of triumph and foreboding.

∼

I TURNED the corner of Ludgate Circus and yanked down the brim of my green felt hat, turning it from a fashion statement into a rather dated cloche. But gusts of wind would not defeat me, and neither would that dreadful shopkeeper. Even after walking two miles from Grosvenor Street, my mind played the horrid scene in a perpetual loop. Perhaps I had imagined the gowns were imitations. Perhaps the shopkeeper was right to show me the door?

I wrinkled my nose at the fluffy Pomeranian scuttling past me, and she responded with a short yap, bounding after her light-footed elderly owner.

"Fina!"

I lifted my eyes and puffed on my fringe. Ruby Dove dashed up to me, as lively as the Pomeranian. Her raven hair was swept up into a jaunty emerald beret, and not a strand was out of place. The circles under her eyes, a likely product of end-of-term late nights at Oxford, had vanished since I'd last seen her, and her cheeks glowed, complementing her favourite opal pinprick earrings and raspberry mouth.

"It's been only a month, but it seems like a year," I said, squeezing her arm. "You look absolutely marvellous. What makeup are you wearing, and where can I purchase it?"

Ruby giggled. "You know they don't carry makeup for my skin-tone. No, I owe my dewy complexion to rest and relaxation at my auntie's, mixed with a dash of good news."

At the words "good news," I gulped. With dawning nervousness, I realised I had to tell her about my troubling discovery in that blasted shop. But that could wait, surely. After all, I wasn't keen on lowering Ruby's spirits. We'd discuss it after tea and maybe a nibble...

"Tell me all about it over tea," I said, pointing to the bustling Lyon's Corner House where we had agreed to meet.

Harried waitresses held their trays high above their heads as customers thronged around them, chattering and clinking their spoons against their teacups. I inhaled the luscious smell of bread, sticky buns, and tea.

"There's a table in the corner." Ruby marched through the crowd of squawking children and a feisty barking terrier. A small child patted the dog, shrieked, and then wobbled backwards, right into my knee. The little blighter grabbed my leg and wiped her pastry-covered mouth on my frock, gleefully seeking my approval as she did so.

"Lizzie, darling, now don't be afraid of the darling doggie," admonished a sturdy woman, clearly little Lizzie Borden's mother. I held my breath, waiting for an apology.

The woman just chewed her currant-bun in a slow, bovine manner. "I say—" I began, but before I could speak, Ruby tugged me away. "It's not worth it, Feens," she hissed. "Besides, I have something that will remove the stain from your frock."

Reluctantly, I followed Ruby to the corner table and plopped down. Despite myself, I grinned.

"What's so funny?" asked Ruby. "You looked like you were about to clobber that frightful child with your bag."

"Oh, nothing. I was just remembering how many times you've had to remove various stains from my clothing. I'd be a positive walking nightmare without you. And not only because of your smashing laundering abilities."

The welcome voice of a waitress interrupted my reverie. "What are you having?" she wheezed.

Her breathy exasperation probably stemmed from her crisp, starched collar and apron strings tighter than a whalebone corset. But her soft, wrinkled smile showed she hadn't let the uniform – or the lunchtime bustle – drain away her good humour.

Ruby removed the grey jacket of her favourite suit and carefully arranged it on the back of her chair. "I'll have tea and a biscuit."

"Tea and a biscuit," the waitress parroted.

I stared at Ruby. Was she on a slimming regime? Even when she'd claimed she'd gained a stone once over Christmas, I never detected any real change. Other than a happier Ruby.

"I'll have a cream tea," I said defiantly – more to myself than to the waitress. "With lashings of cream, please."

"Right you are. Tea and a biscuit and a cream tea."

"With lashings of cream, please," I repeated.

The waitress finished scribbling and sailed toward the kitchen as if she were strolling through a sunny, quiet meadow.

"Aren't you hungry? Are you slimming?" I asked.

"Pish." Ruby waved a hand. "Slimming regimes are not for me...except that one Christmas. No, I'm far too excited to eat. But do tell me how you've been keeping after a entire month!"

I peered out the window, letting my eyes unfocus into the blur of jostling bodies outside. Yes, I'd tell her later, as there was surely no reason to spoil our tea and Ruby's good mood. "I'm too hungry to remember – and I'm certain it's tiresome compared to your news."

Ruby slipped her hand into her black clutch and removed a brown envelope. She slid it across the table, tapping it with a perfectly manicured finger.

"Go on. Read it," she said.

It was a cheque. For £87! Triple that amount would buy a house in London. Or, even more appealing, thousands of Melba chocolate bars. I unfolded the accompanying letter and read it aloud.

Dear Miss Dove:

Thank you for submitting your designs to the House of Lafitte. We've selected two items for inclusion in our new summer-autumn line. Though we are unable to fund travel, we'd be most honoured if you joined us for our private event on April 30th. If you are able to join us, please respond and we will forward the relevant details.

Yours sincerely,

Yvette Jourdain
Executive Partner

House of Lafitte

I LOOKED up from the letter and blinked, unable to take it in. Travel? A private event?

Ruby squeezed my hand. "Don't you see, Feens? We're going to Paris!"

Click to continue reading soon!

MORE MYSTERIES

The Ruby Dove Mystery Series follows the early adventures of our intrepid amateur-spy sleuths:

Book 1: The Mystery of Ruby's Sugar
Book 2: The Mystery of Ruby's Smoke
Book 3: The Mystery of Ruby's Stiletto
Book 4: The Mystery of Ruby's Tracks
Book 5: The Mystery of Ruby's Mistletoe
Book 6: The Mystery of Ruby's Roulette
Book 7: The Mystery of Ruby's Mask
Ruby Dove Mysteries Box Set 1
Ruby Dove Mysteries Box Set 2

With many cases under their fashionable belts, Ruby and Fina are ready for more in *Partners in Spying Mysteries:*

Fatal Festivities: A Christmas Novella
Book 1: Death in Velvet

ABOUT THE AUTHOR

Rose Donovan is a lifelong devotee of golden age mysteries. She now travels the world seeking cosy spots to write, new adventures to inspire devious plot twists, and adorable animals to petsit.

www.rosedonovan.com
rose@rosedonovan.com
Reader Group
Follow me on Bookbub
Follow me on Goodreads

NOTE ABOUT UK STYLE

Readers fluent in US English may believe words such as "fuelled", "signalled", "hiccough", "fulfil", "titbit", "oesophagus", "blinkers", and "practise" are typographical errors in this text. Rest assured this is simply British spelling. There are also spacing and punctuation formatting differences, including periods after quotation marks in certain circumstances.

If you find any errors, I always appreciate an email so I can correct them! Please email me at rose@rosedonovan.com. Thank you!

Printed in Great Britain
by Amazon